SHIPS AGAINST THE SEA

Alan Easton

NIMBUS
PUBLISHING
LIMITED

Tom Dean

Published by: Nimbus Publishing Limited
                   P.O. Box 9301, Station A
                   Halifax, N.S.   B3K 5N5

Design by J.W. Johnson
Typesetting: Atlantic Typesetting Studio
Printing and Binding: Seaboard Printing
Halifax, N.S.

Cover Photo: Michael Chisholm

Canadian Cataloguing in Publication Data

Easton, Alan, 1902 — Ships against the sea
ISBN 0-920852-56-4

1. Sea stories, Canadian. I. Title.
G525.E38 1986   910.4'53   C86-094298-8

Contents

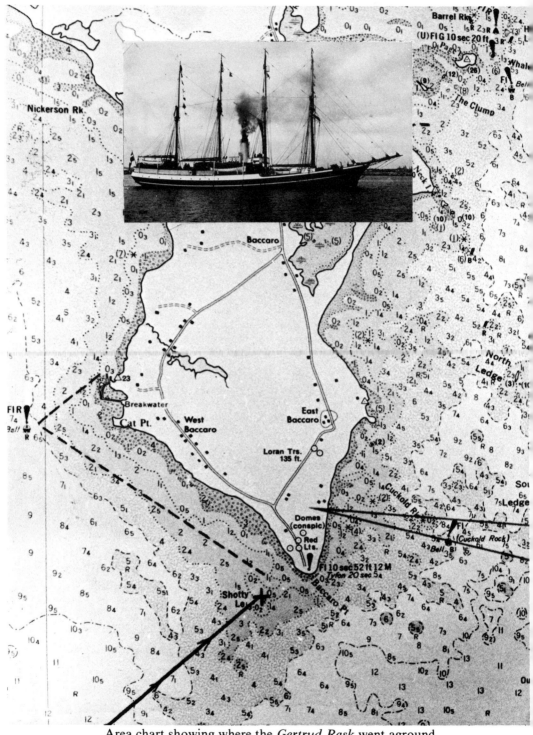

Area chart showing where the *Gertrud Rask* went aground.
Inset: *Gertrud Rask* leaving Copenhagen.

Rescue
at
Dawn

As the sea wears stone into pebbles, so it erodes ships it draws to self. The only evidence that a ship had ever been lost at Baccaro Point ere three blackened timbers some fifteen feet long, still pinned together by eel spikes, lying imbedded and immovable in the sand where the narrow b ch meets the tussocky grass of the foreshore. They were heavy timb rs, impregnated here and there with white streaks of salt, their once jagged er s, where they had been torn away, worn smooth by the incessant surf. 1 e desolate objects spoke of a vessel which had once missed her way or be driven ashore on the rock-studded coast of Nova Scotia.

The *Gertrud Rask* was on a voyage from New York to Holstenbor Greenland, alone—which was unusual in the year 1942. But she could no travel in convoy because she depended on sail for her power. She had ar engine, a tripple expansion steam engine, but of only fifty-eight nominal horse power.

She was a four-masted wooden schooner and had been built in Denmark nineteen years earlier for the Royal Danish Greenland Trading Company. So that she would be protected against ice along the rugged coast on which she was to spend most of her life, her hull, from keel to deep water line, was put together with immensely heavy planking. In profile she was the image of sturdiness yet her lines had grace as well as the impression of strength, her 155 foot length lending itself to these convictions.

A figure-head adorned her out-reaching bow and resembled the woman whose name the vessel honoured. Gertrud Rask was famous in Greenland history. She had followed her husband, a renowned priest, to the remote colony in 1721 and together their ministry had become a legend.

After seventy voyages between Denmark and Greenland the *Gertrud Rask* left Copenhagen for the last time under the command of Captain N.C. Vestmar. It was March 20, 1940. Three weeks later the Germans invaded Denmark so that she could not return. Thenceforward she continued to care for the inhabitants of Greenland; and because of her people's need she went to New York in the dangerous winter of 1942, the height of the German submarine campaign. She carried fish oil in barrels which provided good money and was returning with general cargo which included among other things, gunny sacking, bolts of cloth, children's winter clothing and warm boots, school exercise books and pencils, and as much bunker coal as she could accommodate.

She had passed close to Fire Island and Montauk Point, steered into Buzzard's Bay and steamed through the Cape Cod canal on her engine. Leaving the American shore she sailed into an easterly gale across the Gulf of Maine to Nova Scotia. Her master wanted to hug the Canadian coast, as he had the United States seaboard where he could, because of the U-boat menace. But to make good a course to the north-east the schooner had to beat every mile of the way. Her engine could do little to hold the 660 ton vessel into the gale, though it helped. Her machinery was intended to take her in and out of harbours and fjords becalmed or beset by fluky winds. But by keeping close in to the coast to avoid the perils of war she was caught by the perils of the sea. Her noble career as a Greenland trader was coming to an end on the rocks of a land far from her northern home.

A fisherman in the village of West Baccaro was the first to see the *Gertrud Rask*, through the spindrift at the end of a wintry day. She was close-hauled, clawing into the vicious gale with all the sail she could carry. Oddly, she had a large funnel between the main and mizzen masts and from it broken smoke whipped flat to the sea. She was a stranger to the man of West Baccaro; and as he stood in the lee of his cottage, watching her through the murk of the fading dusk, he knew she was too close in. He feared her captain might not see or hear the whistle buoy of the Bantam Rocks through the dirt to windward, or might not recognize, as he himself would, the ominous flying spray that warned of the Bantams.

She must have weathered Cape Sable, the southern tip of Nova Scotia, but not Brazil Rock; she must have sailed inside it, he reasoned, which was all right for a vessel meaning to keep on the coast. But if she were going to clear Cape Negro she would need to go about. Perhaps she would turn and run for Barrington Bay if it was shelter she was seeking.

The fisherman did not have her long in sight; she faded under the darkening sky; and the onset of night, the night of February 7, was proclaimed by the flash of the lighthouse.

The man outside went in. But being apprehensive he kept a watch to seaward from his stoop. Misgivings on a night like this, cold with a tendency to rain, and the smoke of his fire puffing now and then out into his parlour, were unpleasant to hold.

The village comprised eight or ten cottages, a hundred yards from the shore, spread along the rutted gravel road which made a circuit of the end of the peninsula. They were all within a mile of the lighthouse at the end of a road which branched off in a spur to the point. Their view of the sea was unobstructed.

Presently, out of the darkness the signal came; a small, rather misty white light falling from the sky. Then another, resembling a shooting star coming down in the sea opposite the village.

The fisherman who had reckoned on the possibility of the unknown vessel falling on foul ground and had been loath to turn his eyes away from the sea, now a series of breaking waves on a black void, knew instantly what the stars meant and instinctively knew the plight the strange schooner was likely to be in. Not only he but others caught a glimpse of the distress signal through their uncurtained windows. Pulling on their rubber suits, the women their heavy coats, they emerged to encounter a full gale. Children were sent off to notify other villagers who might have missed the signal. The inclination of the men was to move upwind towards the point. They were right. Suddenly a distant whistle came down wind, the deep-throated whistle of a steamer, swelling and fading in the concussion of the storm. It came again as they hurried on. Searching seaward all now saw another pair of rockets burst, this time at the beginning of their trajectory. They knew they had been shot from projectors; they had risen like fire-crackers to explode almost over the ship. The two stars appeared high above Shotty Ledge, a shallow reef a quarter of a mile out from the shore and directly beneath the beam of Baccaro Light. They drifted to leeward, and disappeared into the sea.

The people struggled along the road in twos and threes, bent against the slanting sleet. They saw a smudge of light beyond the point and as they came down the incline onto the beach the lights filtered through the wet air quite sharply and marked the vessel as being unmistakably on Shotty Ledge. But they faded periodically. She was evidently being enveloped by spray, sometimes by the sea itself, as it broke on the ledge a couple of fathoms beneath the surface. The wavering voice of her whistle, the cry of need, cut into the hearts of the fisherfolk as the driving sleet cut their faces. They knew her plight exactly. But there seemed nothing they could do.

Most of the villagers were gathered on the beach and to communicate they shouted into one another's ears and gesticulated. It was difficult to stand and some put their backs to the wind and watched sideways. The sea was roaring in on the slim stretch of sand and the spindrift from the wave-tops as the cross wind caught them stung too as it curved to leeward.

Uppermost in their minds was the chance that the crew might abandon ship and attempt to bring their lifeboats through the surf. It was not the surf itself which offered the greatest hazard, wild as it was, it was the projecting rocks beneath. Even if the seamen were skilled enough to row in through such a running sea, and it was doubtful if anyone could, they could hardly escape the jagged bottom; it was by no means all sand. But the captain of the stranded vessel would not know this. And the fishermen had no signal light to inform him of the danger, or even to tell him that they had seen his ship. As for launching a boat from the shore it was not even thought of. In any case there were no boats here to launch.

Unfortunately there was no government lifeboat at Baccaro Point or anywhere near. On this long coast fishermen served as the rescuers of crews of foundering ships; they accepted it as their humane duty. And in these times of sea warfare their task had been doubled. Only two weeks ago the *Empire Kingfisher* had been torpedoed off-shore and some of her crew saved from this very ledge by one of the men now on the beach. Shipwrecked seamen had been taken into cottages up and down the shore and given succour as long as they needed it. But in the case of the *Gertrud Rask* they could not get out to her.

The breeches-buoy, a form of rescue sometimes used, could not be employed here; there were no high cliffs from which to suspend a rope. The wreck, moreover, was too far out to shoot a line.

It was no use doing nothing. Word must be passed to the authorities in the hope perhaps that they could reach the vessel from seaward. Someone raeed away with what speed he could to convey the message. He reached his truck and drove it the three miles to Port La Tour and telephoned the naval station at Shelburne, twenty-five miles away. He also notified the Royal Canadian Mounted Police at Barrington Passage.

But the naval station at the outport possessed few ships. There were only three alongside the wharf: the tug *St. Anne*, formerly used for towing lumber rafts in the pulp industry but not truly a sea-going tug; the twenty-six-year old armed yacht *Renard*, small and, though built on destroyer lines, was lightly constructed with a gun on her foc's'le which disturbed her stability; and the old cable ship *Lady Laurier* now engaged mainly in buoy-laying.

When the staff officer in charge of the station listened to the man at Port La Tour he quickly grasped the situation of the unknown ship, and understood why the locals could attempt nothing in the stormy conditions. He told the man to hold on—an urgent message had just been put before him relayed from the Halifax naval radio office. It was an SOS which seemed to emanate from the vessel in question.

While not placing her in as definite a position as the man on the telephone put her, it obviously told of the same shipwreck, and he saw from the signal that the danger her captain felt she was in was serious in the extreme. This confirmed local opinion. Her identity was now made known, though the name *Gertrud Rask* meant nothing to him.

Commander Carr was a quick thinker. He told the man, still on the telephone, that he would send a tug out at once, to which the man replied that, if the weather improved sufficiently, a boat would rendezvous with the tug off the Bantam whistle buoy; they might work together. Then the commander radioed the *Gertrud Rask* through Halifax that a tug was coming to her assistance.

Captain Vestmar would now know that at least those who might be able to save his crew were not unaware of his predicament though they might not know how desperate it was.

Blinding snow was blowing into Shelburne harbour on a whole gale when the staff officer ordered the tug *St. Anne* out to sea with instructions to her captain to proceed to Baccaro Point and use his judgement when he got there. He ordered HMCS *Renard* to follow her. He would have sent the *Lady Laurier* too but for her deckload of buoys; it would have been too dangerous for her to face the gale outside with such an unwieldy cargo.

Three mounted policemen from the Shelburne detachment drove down the peninsula and met the constable from Barrington Passage. There was no Marine Division as there had been; the navy had absorbed it at the beginning of the war. But the force ashore on the coast was ready to perform any task. They were a stalwart body of men who seemed to shrink from nothing.

So by ten o'clock that night they joined the local inhabitants who were guarding the beach.

It was an unhappy scene. The fishermen, used to the weather, leaned into the driving rain and sleet and, powerless, watched through screwed-up eyes as the lights on the ship faded while wave after wave covered her. They moved about unsteadily, buffeted by the gusts of wind, keeping a watch on the ugly sea for what it might throw up.

In his official report the police constable from Barrington Passage wrote: "Due to the heavy rain and howling gale it was impossible to stand on the beach for any length of time. In order to keep a constant watch on the ship a detail was made up where members of the force were posted on the rocks and relieved at half hour intervals. It was considered that if the crew abandoned the ship they would need every possible aid to drag them out of the breakers..." Since the members of the force numbered only four it was a thin detail. The fishermen were relieving one another in the same way and taking shelter at the lighthouse.

Whatever may have been smashed aboard the schooner or blown away, the radio aerial must still have been intact. A message received at Shelburne asked when the tug would reach them. They were told 0100. Shortly after midnight a further signal was received: "Cannot wait. Shall abandon ship."

This was the drastic move the staff officer hoped the captain would not decide to make. He was in telephone communication with Port La Tour and was fully aware of the weather conditions. He scribbled an answer and was given priority for its dispatch: "Remain by your ship. Await rescue from seaward. Tug on way. Any attempt to land will invite instant destruction of boats and loss of life. Treacherous shore."

At Baccaro it was judged that the *Gertrud Rask* had gone aground soon after high water and that she was on the outer edge of Shotty. She could not have run far onto the ledge itself because at that stage of the tide there would have been only about 10 feet of water over it; and the schooner, from what had been seen of her, would have drawn more than that. Nor would she be swept further onto it or over it and drift towards the beach; in fact, it was not much deeper inside the shoal. As the hours passed and the tide fell she would be wedged tighter, making her more immovable; and with her hull becoming further exposed she would offer greater resistance to the sea and feel more intensely its crushing power.

To the observers on shore, peering through the misty darkness, catching now and then in the beam of the powerful flash from the lighthouse a sheet of spray punched from an arrested wave flying high over the derelict, it seemed as though she could not stand against it much longer. Their lifelong familiarity with the destructive force of a charging sea told the fishermen that all the lighter gear must be washed away, hatches stove in, the hull strained and opening, her back probably broken. For those abandoned souls on board it would be terrifying; for those ashore it was heartbreaking, defeating.

There were only five fishing boats operating on the peninsula, three on the east side, two on the west—the others had been hauled up for the winter— but their skippers knew they could not put off, much less survive on Shotty.

Their sympathy and their fear for those of their own kind in distress caught in their throats more often than the wind.

The ship was now in darkness. And it did not help when a moan came from the steam whistle, sounding like a dying gasp. It was probably the whistle lanyard tautening under the pressure of the gale.

A naval signalman had been sent down and this had established local communication by lamp. It had been spasmodic but the ship at least knew that there were people on the beach. Perhaps the captain would have to rely on them. At this hour, two o'clock in the morning, it must have been apparent to him that the tug would not be able to get close enough to help them. The *St. Anne*, in fact, was never to arrive. She had turned back after struggling for several hours, unable to weather the storm outside Shelburne harbour. The little *Renard* had to return sooner; the gale, with sleet and icing, was altogether too much for her.

About four o'clock flares were seen to flicker, filtering through the murk fitfully. Ashore it was feared they were attempting to launch a boat, more likely a raft, yet how men could stand on deck to do so was not understood. The signalman was told to flash a warning that they faced certain death if they took to rafts or boats. "Hold on till daylight," they were urged. From where he was standing black rocks shone in the beam of his Aldis lamp as the white water receded with the undertow. They were not informed that the tug had turned back. Nor was a question asked about the tug again.

Once more a message passed across the water. It was about an hour after the flares had gone out. It merely stated: "Ship full of water. Cannot stay much longer." To which an answer was sent: "An attempt at rescue will be made at daylight if wind drops."

Presently the lamp flickered again from the schooner, her final signal: "Will try to wait for you."

A sense of relief was felt when the signalman translated the language of the lamp to the bystanders. It made them impatient too for the morning light but it was mixed with apprehension.

A little before dawn what had been hoped for seemed to occur. The wind moderated and veered to the south-east and the rain ceased. Those who were sheltering at the lighthouse came down the sandy track again to the edge of the beach; some women were among them, several boys. After a while a further decrease in the strength of the wind was noticed and it veered still more to the south. But with the change came fog. The damp drifting vapour diffused the powerful light that flashed above them and brought on the raucous blare of the fog horn.

Fog was a good omen; it was seldom accompanied by gale force winds. Some optimism pervaded the group, a characteristic not often evident among fisherfolk. And they no longer had to yell to be heard though the waves still thundered in and the horn interrupted their laconic speech.

Skipper Douglas Smith, the man who had rescued the survivors of the *Empire Kingfisher*, decided that at the first thread of light he would try to get out of Smithsville, a cove two miles up the east side protected by Crow

Neck Island. His was one of the five operational boats. Two other men joined him as did the staff officer who had arrived sometime earlier from Shelburne. After warming up the engine and making ready with plenty of rope they left the wharf and plunged into the fog.

Though rocks surrounded them there was a clear passage out and Smith knew his way. He soon knew he had passed the lee of Crow Neck; his twenty-eight-foot boat rose into the breakers. He was swept back, almost broaching to. The skipper steered into the shifting foam again. Unable to see more than three boat's lengths in the dim dawn and dense fog he felt his way into the wind. He drove into the waves again and again, burying the boat, rising and facing the crests. But it was no use, he could not get out. Smith had to put his stern to the dying gale but not yet dying sea.

Back on the beach under the lighthouse the fishermen and police keeping watch on the water found, as the grey dawn crept over the scene, that, much to their disappointment, the wreck was hidden in the fog. They had hoped the atmosphere would have been clear enough to see her—and appraise her plight. All that was visible was a short stretch of sea still running in fast from behind the misty backdrop. But the lessening spindrift confirmed their audible conviction that the wind was lulling. It was now blowing from the south-west.

Several men broke away. They took the path up to the road and trudged through the puddles towards West Baccaro. Children up early in the village asked where they were going and when told followed close behind. They went over the coarse brown grass that still bowed to the wind that blew across the treeless land, and made for their tiny harbour beside Cat Point. Few words passed between them as they stood on the little rise above the wharf, spray belching over the breakwater often blinding their view and rattling like hail on the roof of the fish shed near them.

Below lay two boats, their owners on the rise anxiously wondering what the prospects were for venturing out. It was the nearest boat harbour to Shotty, a mile and a half distant by sea. They asked themselves two questions: Had the might of the surf been subdued enough by the falling tide to allow a boat to survive? The ebb normally quietened it. And was the tide at a safe level to leave the harbour mouth? Conditions had to balance—if they would balance. It was half-tide now; some thought too late to go.

The skippers, Fred Chetwynd and Sydney Christie, thought the wind was still dropping. Their volunteer crews agreed. Others came to the dock to assess the skippers' chances. They were thought to be slim. They had to consider what failure would bring. To capsize or to be holed by the rocks was to drown or be crushed.

Though the observers no longer inclined their bodies towards the wind, their clothes only fluttering now, the momentum of the sea could not be expected to diminish as quickly as the gale dwindled. Yet there was a difference in the sea; the men could see that. The spray at times, as the waves broke or collided with one another, was thrown up to hang tremulously and fall, rather than drive shorewards. But this occurred only in the lulls.

West Baccaro harbour had little natural protection. It was a small artificial haven enclosed by a sea-wall built on the rocks close to Cat Point, a low promontory, which afforded almost no lee. Most of it dried out at low tide into rocky ground leaving the usable area a narrow finger of water protected by the breakwater. It had the unfavourable feature of being shallow both inside and out at low water which made it dangerous to attempt to enter at any stage below half tide in rough weather. The hazard was the rocks that studded the bottom beyond the mouth. On the other hand in a heavy sea and strong onshore wind fishermen would neither approach nor leave it at high water. It was a harbour with grave restrictions.

The fog in its fickle way thinned; the assembled company, in rubber suits and high boots, saw the sea stretching farther back. It was a white seething tract out to the misty deeper water. The two skippers moved restlessly about the gravelly ground above the dock looking in different directions and at the low skudding clouds overhead but mainly along the line of the invisible bell buoy beyond the five-fathom line.

Still they waited, though the ebb had been running for more than three hours. Haste was needed yet they could not hasten. Fred Chetwynd, tall, slim, in his early thirties, had fished out to this harbour always. Christie had done so perhaps a little longer. All who stood there knew the waters around Baccaro: they had grown from boyhood to know the deeps and banks and rocks.

Fear did not invade Skipper Chetwynd's heart: he was unmoved by the sight of the cruel sea. Though he often put himself in the hands of Providence he could also rely on his sea-sense, as an experienced motorist depends on his road-sense on a snowy highway. Suddenly he spoke to a man near him. "Start my engine, Danny, and run her a bit." Danny Bower went down to the wharf followed by Julius Purdy and Rodman Brannan.

The fog cleared to the buoy; they could see the lantern structure swaying like a sapling. It was the sea now—not so much the wind or fog.

"I'm going," Chetwynd announced at last, his eyes, blue as the sea, still focused on the surging harbour mouth. Skipper Christie, standing next to him, surveyed the perilous conditions once more, then nodded. They went down to the only two boats still afloat on the West Shore. Sydney Christie took two men, Earl Christie and Cecil Chetwynd—names repeated themselves in the neighbourhood.

The villagers, standing on the rise above the dock, watched the twenty-eight-foot cape island boat with its long sea-going sheer and protective deck extending from bow to pilot shelter, glide down the strip of calm water, Chetwynd hardly turning his wheel. He had to keep close to the stone breakwater, the entrance was narrowed still further by boulders. Then the thump of the motor's exhaust resounded above the noise of the waves as he swung round the end, heeled to the first blow, righted and mounted the incoming sea. The boat dived out of sight behind the breakwater, then came into view as it rose into the breakers again.

The onlookers dug their fingers into their hands and drew their breath in each time Chetwynd pitched down into the shallows, fearful he would strike the sandy bottom, or worse, a projecting rock. Some were down nearer the water's edge ready to urge the swimmers to shore if the hull was pierced—though swimming in such clothes as they wore would have been almost impossible.

But the boat still forged ahead, the skipper's course being determined by the direction of the sea. He struck through the surf, buried in spray, lifted and plunged...to rise again and face crest after arched crest of curving rollers.

The eyes of those ashore left Chetwynd half way through the surf to watch Skipper Christie throw his heavy boat round the end of the dock and stand out to sea. Instantly she reared skywards and some feared she would be thrown back. In a welter of spume she staggered out, then rolled and showed her keel. He held her up and into the onslaught; he knew his boat. They could still see the crew crouching as the craft battled on, sometimes through, sometimes over the crests of the running sea. Christie's boat did not ground either.

The two boats cleared the surf and reached the bell buoy. But there the swell, the legacy of the gale, was high and steep. In turning, one behind the other towards Shotty Ledge, they had to ride half sideways up the hillocks. The men gripped what was handy and watched the ever-changing contour through their pilot shelter windows.

When half way along their course they saw the *Gertrud Rask* shrouded like a phantom in the thinning mist. She gradually became clearer until she stood black against the dull grey background. The eyes of all seven men in the boats fastened on the confused water around her. That was the vital element. Though the sea was breaking heavily over the ledge, racing and swirling, foam-streaked across it, it was not pounding the vessel's hull as it obviously had in the night gale and flood tide. But green water still washed over her decks periodically. She stood unnaturally high and had a list to starboard, probably in conformity with the ground she was resting on. Some sails were furled; she may have lost others.

As the fishermen drew nearer she looked gaunt in her stillness, lonely and pathetic like a torn sea-bird. They marvelled that she had not broken in two. Flotsam was tossing to leeward; her hatches had been opened to the sea. No one could be below, yet who could stay on deck—for long!

A few more minutes and they saw the crew. They were in the rigging, the fore and mizzen.

The noise was thunderous on the reef. Even so, at the sea's indrawn breath between the breakers the higher pitched outcry of the nearby surf racing in towards the lighthouse could be heard by the men in the boats, who now sought a way to close the derelict.

Both boats lay between the two hazards and when they eased their motors to approach the ledge they drifted quickly towards the surf. Each tried his own tactics. There was ample water on the ledge for a motor boat but it was so rough and swift that it was extremely difficult to manoeuvre without swamping the after end and submerging the engine box. When they headed out after drifting towards shore the spray they shipped made it difficult to see.

Chetwynd fell back twice but finally came within fifty yards of the *Gertrud Rask*. During his approaches he had observed the hands coming down the rigging. Now he saw that the starboard lifeboat amidships, the lee boat, which was swung out, was manned and fully occupied.

Suddenly she was in the water, cut lose and free. No signals had passed; the noise was too great for a voice to be heard; actions were enough, they were obvious to seamen.

Instantly under oars she was swept away from the side of the schooner, swung round heading into the sea and drifted against the pull of the oars. There seemed to be about twelve in the boat of whom eight were pulling.

Chetwynd watched for a moment, his engine running half speed, then under a firm hand he manoeuvered his boat to meet the other. He glanced back. One of his men already had the coils of a heaving line in his hands.

He strove to lessen the gap as the tossing lifeboat, catching sheets of spray, dropped back. The rope went out to windward of its destination. It curved as it uncoiled, thrown by a fisherman with the skill of a marksman, and fell across the lifeboat.

With a wave of his arm the man payed out the heavier tow rope as those in the lifeboat hauled it in. Chetwynd had to stop his engine to prevent the rope fouling the propeller and the cape islander fell broadside on and wallowed.

When the hand signal came that the lifeboat had made fast the two were down on the edge of the surf. Taking up the slack of the rope Chetwynd opened his throttle, the motor roared and he forged clear.

There were others still aboard. Skipper Christie lay off as best he could in about the same position as Chetwynd had. He guessed they had gone to the weather lifeboat on the port side; the after one on the lee quarter looked too small to withstand the sea.

To launch the weather boat with water still flooding over the vessel could only be done by experienced sailors, in this case Arctic seamen accustomed to boatwork. And to pull away would require great strength, much of which must have been sapped from their bodies while clinging half frozen to the rigging.

But the second lifeboat appeared around the bow of the wreck. Christie drove forward to intercept her. He took her in tow, having the same struggle to keep out of the surf, and set off for the bell buoy.

They left behind a torn and gutted vessel; not a living soul aboard that they could see.

Skipper Chetwynd hesitated to take his tow in when he reached the buoy; he was fearful of losing control of her at the harbour entrance—if he ever got as far as that. Though time had already run out he idled his motor and gazed at the surf. He glanced back along the tow rope and at the water. The wind had fallen away; the wave-tops had dwindled but the swell was high though not much ruffled.

He made up his mind. Anchoring the lifeboat he came alongside it and, in spite of the crashing and grinding, he transferred the crew to his own boat. This accomplished without injury he swung round and headed into the surf.

It was now two hours before low water and although the ebb had somewhat tranquillized the sea's vicious inrush it left it shallower closer in. Those ashore who had witnessed the rescue on Shotty Ledge and had followed the boats along the coast waited at the harbour to see them return. Much fear was felt. For a hundred yards out the depth at this stage of the tide was only about eight feet making the rocks and boulders inhabiting the bottom perilously close to the surface in the troughs.

Fred Chetwynd came in fast in order to keep steerage way but even so the waves overtook his boat. The buoyant stern of the square transomed cape islander lifted to the oncoming breakers she could not outrun, her bow pointing steeply downhill, and took the curling tops aboard. He gripped the wheel and his breathing came faster as he neared the breakwater—but she did not strike. When his bow pitched up on the back of an overtaking wave his boat seemed to glide backwards into the valley astern and he waited for the rudder to touch, but it did not.

Yawing, yet still under steering control, Chetwynd swept down on the crevice he had to enter. Judging the power of his engine and his drift he threw his wheel hard over to make his last manoeuvre. Her bow responded to her rudder slowly, frighteningly slowly, then gave in. The boat heeled far over in a trough, rounded the stone wall and shot into calm water.

A cheer went up ashore.

Skipper Sydney Christie saw the anchored lifeboat at the bell buoy and knew what his partner had done. He could not stay to do the same, he must go in now. He thought of waiting for the next tide to try it at higher water, but he reckoned the survivors could not wait five hours. Furthermore the tide would be flooding then and perhaps the wind would be blowing again.

He disliked what he was about to do yet he turned his craft and faced the land.

His men shortened the tow-rope which was as risky as it was advantageous but Christie saw the difficulty of hauling the lifeboat around the knuckle of the breakwater and into the narrow gut.

He could not go fast through the surging sea and the breakers came over the stern. It was as bad or worse for the lifeboat. He saw her several times when she topped the waves and his boat was also high; she seemed to be following like a crab. In the welter of movement he could feel the jar of the tow-rope as it took up the strain of the yaw. Manila was strong but he knew rope could part.

Christie's concern was his tow; he forgot about the boulders beneath him. The lifeboat was taking water but swamping would not sink her; buoyancy tanks would keep her afloat. He thought once he saw them bailing. Then she seemed to be travelling faster than he was—surfing.

Christie came down close to the end of the breakwater, as close as he dared. He swung around it and gained the still water. But he did not stop. He intended to pull the lifeboat in before she fell against the rocky shore. Looking back he saw they had the oars out. As the tow-rope turned the lifeboat the men at the oars arrested her drift and Christie hove her in through the gap.

A cheer came once more from the onlookers as they ran down to help the survivors onto the wharf. Few people had seen the harbour made at such a state of sea and tide, or with a greater display of seamanship.

All hands had been rescued. None came to harm though they had suffered severely from the cold, particularly as most of them had been wet for a long time. Captain Vestmar had saved his crew by holding out; the fishermen by going forward saved them all: the master, twenty-three seamen and a passenger. Four were Eskimos, one a girl of seventeen though no one recognized her to be a female. They were warmed and dried in the fishermen's homes and then taken to Shelburne where they were given accommodation. None needed medical attention.

Much relief was felt in West Baccaro for the men's safe return, a village used to living with the sense of deliverance. The men who went out were not those whose courage was a reflex action without time to think. Their's was the courage of men who saw the grim thing they faced and had plenty of time to avoid it, yet went inflexibly into it.

A calm descended on the ocean the next day. Skipper Douglas Smith took the police out to the *Gertrud Rask* and recovered three bags of mail and about a million Danish crowns which were returned to the captain. Much of the cargo had been washed out of her through the broken hatches. As it drifted ashore it was born away by the Receiver of Wrecks who was appointed to take charge of the vessel.

Also on this day the RCMP reported: "Two constables remained on board assisting in keeping unauthorized persons from boarding the vessel." They were assisting the army. Commander Carr in his report said: "The Cape Sable Islanders cannot understand why they are not permitted to plunder a wreck. They made such a determined attempt to loot the *Gertrud Rask* that it was necessary to send a bren gun section to the ship and to fire several bursts before the twenty odd fishing boats from the Island were driven off."

The men of Baccaro had no objection to this. They were not in favour of their friends across the bay attempting to claim what would be theirs when official interest dissolved.

Commander Carr went on in his report: "They will risk their own lives to rescue the crew of a vessel in distress and open their hearts and their homes to victims of the sea, but they cannot understand why a wreck itself is not legitimate spoil." Those on the coast of the Maritimes had always been interested in wrecks. It was just logical salvage.

Captain Vestmar paid a last sad visit to his ship and then went to New York with his crew to purchase another vessel.

For two weeks the *Gertrud Rask* stood fast on Shotty Ledge. Then another wild storm struck the coast and she was dislodged and carried by the high tides over the ledge and up onto the beach. There she remained for several years until the sea took all but three blackened timbers.

At the time the news of the wreck was not published; none was in those wartime days. After the war it was obscure history. Yet the episode was not entirely forgotten. In 1945 the fishermen who crewed in the three boats received King George V's Commendation as a mark of appreciation. The skippers, including Douglas Smith who tried and failed, were awarded the British Empire Medal, a silver disk suspended from a clasp of oak leaves on a rose-pink ribbon edged with pearl-grey. Beneath Britannia it bore the motto, 'For Meritorious Service.'

The Derelict

Summer fog lay on the edge of the Grand Banks of Newfoundland. The corvette HMCS Sackville, crept slowly towards something hidden yet known to be on the quiet sea. For a moment a dark impression smudged the grey mist where it met the water; then as suddenly the black hull of a ship revealed itself in the early morning light.

I glanced instinctively at her waterline. No bow-wave fell away from her forefoot. She was motionless. *Sackville*, one of many Canadian naval ships on the Atlantic, approached her side. The freighter gave the appearance of being heavily laden with her bow deep and a list to port. She was not old; obviously a war-built ship. Her stunted fore-and main-masts and her thin signal-mast amidships made her singularly unattractive, and her untidy state added to her ugliness.

There was no visible damage, but then, a torpedoed ship often hid her wounds. She was not a unique casualty in this year of 1942 when upwards of a hundred allied ships a month were being sunk.

Her decks were deserted; there was no one on the bridge, nor the usual familiar figure at the galley door. One lifeboat on the port side was gone, the other was lying in the water hooked to its forward rope fall; the after block was dangling in the water. A raft was drifting alongside. I picked up a megaphone. "Ship ahoy," I hailed, repeating it several times up and down the ship. My shouts echoed back with a flat, dismal hollowness but there was no reply. The black ship seemed empty and dead, a melancholy phantom on a lifeless sea overhung by fog.

Sackville steamed around the bow. The heavy paravane booms, formed like a bastard bowsprit, stood out at a drooping angle conforming to her low-lying fo'c'sle head.

No damage could be seen on the starboard side either. One of her lifeboats was still at its davits, griped to its boom as though ready to withstand a winter gale; the other lying water-logged alongside, hooked on to its falls. As on the other side a large raft lay farther aft attached by a long line to the main rigging.

Her stern was high, the upper part of her rudder exposed and a bronze propeller blade stood out of the water like a finger pointing to the sky. She gave the impression of wanting to plunge slowly and silently head first to

The S.S. *Belgian Soldier* torpedoed and abandoned.

the bottom, a hundred fathoms below. No name or port of registry was painted on the overhanging counter—it was wartime.

In the quiet of the breathless air a cry came suddenly from beyond the impenetrable veil somewhere astern of the derelict. It came again, the voice of distress sensing, perhaps, the faint sound of water parted by a slowly moving vessel. But the corvette passed on, ignoring it. The stricken ship had first claim.

Coming up her port side once more a figure was seen on deck. A man stood outside the 'midship accommodation. The solitary black image was dressed in an overcoat and a civilian hat as though he was about to go ashore. He held a suitcase in each hand.

"Are you the only man aboard?" I shouted.

He called something that could not be heard clearly. Questioned again, he put his suitcases down carefully, cupped his hands around his mouth and shouted, "Yes," and some unintelligible words.

The boarding party rowed across to the all but abandoned ship, climbed the rope ladder which hung dejectedly down the side, swung aboard. I now took the corvette back into the fog whence the cry for help had come.

The splash of condensing fog-drops were audible as they fell from the yard and struck the deck. The appealing voice was there again—somewhere. It rose and fell beyond the small visible circle of glassy ocean. Then vaguely the object took shape. Almost instantly, with startling clarity a boat was unlatched from the fog.

The single occupant of the large lifeboat was balancing himself precariously on a thwart, one hand on a pump, the other held above his head as through in greeting. Closing the distance, he was heard singing snatches of something that sounded like a spiritual as he applied a few strokes to the pump, evidently as a matter of habit. He never took his eyes off the approaching corvette, even as he went on his knees and, losing his balance, toppled back into the water-filled boat. He was very cold when he was brought on board, his wet clothes grasping his strong black body. Shivering violently he collapsed on the deck and sobbed.

"What are her chances?" I asked the officer in charge of the boarding party when the corvette returned to the derelict and picked them up.

"Fair if the sea holds calm," he answered. "She might stay afloat for a week. She was steady enough."

"She'll be torpedoed again if it clears and she's seen. Damage?"

"No. 3 hatch blown out and flooded below. Maybe No. 2 is partly filled too. Engine-room has some water in it and no doubt the stokehold. She's an almighty shambles on deck."

"Any confidential books or codes left aboard?" I asked.

"Yes. They weren't thrown overboard. We have them. Seemed as though an attempt had been made to collect them but they'd been dropped—in a hurry."

"Panic, I wonder?"

"Maybe. Looked like a hasty abandonment."

"What's her name?"

"Not sure," the officer replied. "I saw the name *Empire Selwyn* but the fireman says she's the *Belgian Soldier*."

I glanced at my convoy list. '*Empire Selwyn*. No. 94. In ballast. Destination, St. Lawrence River.'.

"In ballast," I murmured. "Partly flooded. Pity they didn't stay by her longer. But I know how it must have felt."

Sackville left her, forlorn, desolate and silent; a more urgent duty called the naval ship. In response to my signalled suggestion a tug was dispatched from Newfoundland to tow her in but she could not be found. No one ever did find her unless it was a U-boat; there were many submarines in the ocean that summer.

The *Empire Selwyn* was built by Doxford in Sunderland in 1941 for the British Ministry of War Transport. Her style was that of a normal cargo ship of World War II except that her bow was reinforced to crush a passage through ice. She measured 7,167 tons gross and was 420 feet long, her speed ten and one-half knots. She was a coal-burning steamer.

Her maiden voyage was made in convoy to Murmansk during February and March, 1942. At about the time of her return to British waters it had been decided that the government would transfer to her allies in exile in England, whose merchant fleets had almost vanished, a number of ships proportional to their losses in the conflict. The *Empire Selwyn* fell to the Belgians and, following the usual custom, was renamed. She became the *Belgian Soldier*.

She was lying empty in Glasgow when her Belgian captain joined her on July 11. Though berthed with other ships on the quayside she alone lay silent without a crew. But within a week the officers had joined her, assigned by the managers, L. Dens and Company, Belgian shipowners in London. And the shipping office had provided a handful of men. Ballast was being poured into the ship before the captain knew his destination. She took 1,200 tons of sand. With her bunkers loaded and her double bottom water ballast tanks full she had a draught of fourteen feet forward and nineteen feet aft which would provide her with a modest grasp of the water for a summer passage and her propeller a fair depth to turn in. Thus the *Belgian Soldier* sailed down the River Clyde on July 18 and anchored at the Tail-of-the-Bank.

But here the master had difficulty in making up the balance of his crew. He waited at the pool-like confluence of the upper and lower reaches of the river for a week, making periodic visits to the crew assembly point at Greenoch. He took aboard his final stores which included several cases of whisky in bond. He tried but could not obtain enough life-jacket lights to serve his entire complement. By a count he was twenty-nine short, short of the little red lights which floated beside a man in the water and by which his position could be seen at night, often his only means of being discovered. Nor were the attendant whistles, the voice of the mariner in such a predicament, in stock at the government stores.

By now the captain knew where he was bound; he had attended the convoy conference composed of the masters of the ships of the Clyde section. The *Belgian Soldier* was to sail for the St. Lawrence River, Montreal probably. This was his first conference; he had not been a shipmaster before. He had spent some twenty years at sea but the *Belgian Soldier* was his first command. He was almost thirty-eight.

Returning from the meeting with his orders he tried to raise steam. But he still lacked enough firemen. By scouring all sources however, the authorities found enough men to make up a crew of fifty-two. But they were an ill-assorted crowd. Nearly half were Belgians—deck officers, engineers and their senior hands, and most of the catering staff. The gunners were English, four of whom were soldiers. The able seamen were French, Portuguese and Belgian whites; the firemen British and Portuguese blacks.

Late that long summer evening the chief officer held a boat drill. Officers and men were divided among the four lifeboats and were told the signal for abandoning the ship—long blasts on the steam whistle. The drill did not include lowering the boats into the water, or even halfway, to practice handling the ropes. The total approved capacity of all boats was 176 and either of the two larger ones would accommodate the whole crew. So there was plenty of room.

The *Belgian Soldier* sailed in company with several other ships at dawn on July 25 to join the westbound Atlantic convoy, 'ON 115.'

It was a brilliant, cloudless morning when the Clyde section emerged at the Mull of Kintyre and fell in with the main body of the convoy out of Liverpool, in the same way as the Milford Haven section had joined it during the night in the Irish Sea. There were now forty-one ships. Coming from the north the Clyde ships took up a position on the starboard side and in doing so extended the formation to nine columns, each column having four or five ships in it. The width across the face of this advancing armada was therefore about four miles and its depth roughly two. It was led by the commodore in No. 51, the leading ship in the centre column. The *Belgian Soldier* bore pennant No. 94; thus she was the fourth and rear ship of the ninth column.

Soon the naval escort was seen coming across from the River Foyle. Pitching and rolling slightly, the sun threw reflecting rays now and then from their damp hulls. They surrounded the convoy. The Mid-Ocean Escort Group was made up of six Canadian ships, two destroyers and four corvettes. They would take this mass of traders across the Western Ocean to the Grand Banks, approximately ten days steaming.

On the *Belgian Soldier* ship routine seemed to the captain to fall into place that afternoon. He devoted his attention to seeing that the officers-of-the-watch kept proper station on the ship ahead and, during the night, did not crowd the ship in the next column. Fortunately it was moonlight and that made it easier. He did not know yet the strength of his officers, their practical aptitudes, the degree of attention they would pay to the navigation and care of the ship. He was glad in a way that his vessel was down in the far corner of the formation clear of all but the ship abeam and not hemmed in on both sides, astern and ahead as were those in the centre. But to be on the outside edge of the convoy and in the rear gave him a feeling of being exposed, unprotected by the hulls of other ships. Yet he knew the centre ships, the tankers, were the most valuable, more so than his, yet his had immense value—every vessel capable of keeping the sea was indispensable at this disastrous stage of the war.

He had talked to the chief officer about security and felt confident he could rely on him to ensure that the ship was darkened at night, that the gunners were on duty, the seamen detailed to stand lookout, and could depend upon him for general upkeep on deck. It was as it should have been.

The night passed uneventfully and the second day dawned fine and clear. The convoy moved forward in good formation over a sea that was barely ruffled and with only a slight south-westerly swell. The captain examined the nearer ships with his binoculars. Most were obviously in ballast, 'flying light' like his own, which was the common condition of west-bound convoys in his experience. The tankers were the deepest; they would have most of their oil tanks filled with saltwater ballast.

The day passed quietly. He was pleased it was tranquil. He slept on his settee in his cabin below the bridge in the afternoon, a pleasant thing but also a precaution against the possible demand for wakefulness at night.

It was shortly after dark that the chief officer, who was making his rounds of the deck, noticed lights shining from two portholes. He found they came from the chief engineer's cabin and the second officer's, both close together. He took it up with them at once, berating the second officer with much vehemence. He could not castigate the chief very severely because he did not have the same jurisdiction over him. He became aware that both had been drinking and had probably opened their ports to seek fresh air.

The captain came onto the bridge as the eastern sky showed signs of morning. The chief officer, who was in charge, remarked that the second engineer's deafness was a serious disadvantage. He had called him by telephone to increase the revolutions as they had fallen back from their station but could not make him understand what was wanted. He had tried the voicepipe with no better success so he sent the fourth officer, who was on watch with him, down to the engine-room to give him the order. The elderly man then carried out the instruction.

In mid-morning the chief engineer informed the captain that the firemen had come to him demanding beer. He had given them some. Was that all right? The captain supposed it was. He could not recall encountering such a request before but then, his recent experiences had been as chief officer and matters concerning the gang in the stokehold had bypassed him; they had been resolved by the chief engineer or in consultation between him and the master.

Towards noon the radio operator appeared on the bridge to say that he had been listening to what he was certain were the medium frequency transmissions of a U-boat. He had occasionally tuned out of the convoy band

and in doing so had picked them up. How far away did he think they were? Close: perhaps even within sight.

The captain became conscious of a return of that feeling which he had so resolutely kept from his mind; a sinking in his heart, the sense of depression. The symptom had appeared more than a year ago and had become almost malignant in his latter ocean crossings. It had been impossible to shake off though he had kept it hidden, and at the end of a voyage it quietened. He was now miserably aware that the old sensation, like the recurrence of a sickening pain, was there. He had hoped that he could stave it off this time, for a while at least, and not allow it to grip him on the first warning of impending danger.

This intelligence made him aware of the purpose, perhaps, of the high speed departure of the two destroyers over the horizon to the north which he had noticed earlier in the morning.

When the noon position of the convoy was passed to all ships by flag hoist from the commodore it agreed closely with his own observations. They were making good progress. And why not? The weather was good.

During the four-eight watch, sometime after the evening meal in the saloon, the chief engineer climbed the ladder to the bridge again. The firemen and trimmers wanted whisky. He had said no. But there was one very obstinate man, a native of Sierra Leone, who had spoken out strongly. The chief knew now that this man was an agitator, he could see it in his demeanour and he felt there was going to be trouble below before the trip was over.

It was unfortunate to the captain's mind that the man who was addressing him spoke through a whisky breath.

When the chief had gone he called the chief steward to his cabin. Not a drinker at sea the captain was sensitive to those who were. He remarked that he hoped the privilege of drinking was not being abused. The steward assured him it was not, and said that he thought these men needed some stimulant since most of them were, even now in these favourable conditions, being reminded of past voyages of great strain and were separated from their families, too, with their country under the domination of the Germans. The captain recognized that the speaker was feeling the strain he spoke of as much as any. He could not blame him.

At five o'clock that afternoon a series of flag hoists fluttered from the yard of the commodore's ship and were repeated by the leading ships of the columns. A turn of 45° to port was ordered for 8:30. There were submarines about, obviously. Perhaps the ships had been sighted. An attempt was now being made to dodge the enemy in darkness—but it would not be a dark night. And the ponderous artifice of turning aside could hardly be called dodging.

On his visits that night to the bridge during the middle watch all appeared well. The second officer was vigilant it seemed and had the vessel on station. Light clouds drifted occasionally across the waning three-quarter moon which threw deceptive shadows on the rippled sea. On such a lighted ocean a tall black ship would stand up like a mountain to a watcher in a low-lying boat. Conversely, to an observer aloft in the big ship, the silver wavelets and the darker hollows of the swell created spectral forms which would tire his sight and sometimes unbalance his judgement.

When the captain came up as day was breaking the chief officer said the ship had dropped back but was catching up now after he had notified the engine-room. They had evidently lost the head of steam after the change of the watch. He went on to say that he had tried to wake the engine-room up by giving a double ring on the telegraph but had had no response. He had sent the fourth officer down as he had several times before and he had been obliged to give the order to the donkeyman because he could not arouse the second engineer.

The critical time of dawn, favoured by U-boat commanders for attacking, passed and the captain went below to sleep fitfully.

The radio operator reported more transmissions which he was sure emanated from more than one submarine.

At noon the chief engineer asked the captain to come down to the after deck. A demand had been made again by the firemen, led by the troublemaker, that whisky be issued to them. The chief could not find the words to cope with it. The captain's English was much better, besides it was advisable that he settled the matter once and for ever. When he attempted to do so, refusing the liquor, the deep voice of the leader became menacing and he was clearly understood by the two Belgians to say, "No whisky, no steam."

At this pronouncement the captain threatened to call over the corvette, which he pointed to a mile or so away to starboard, and arrest the men who refused to fire the furnaces. This stilled the ringleader and the two half-naked blacks with him grinned sheepishly.

But in the course of gaining the upper hand something unexpected became evident to the captain from the argument put up by the spokesman about the heavy work they had to do. The watertight doors in the bulkhead between the stokehold and No. 3 hold must have been open at night.

When the agitator and his companions were dismissed the captain asked the chief engineer why he had permitted the doors to remain open, apparently for twenty-four hours a day. The chief replied that it was easier to take the coal out direct from No. 3 into the stokehold than trim it out of the side bunkers. It was not quite a question of ease of handling, the captain argued, it was a question of safety. All ships shut these watertight doors and dogged them tight at night, even if they had taken coal through the doors in daytime, the chief knew that. He had better make sure they were shut in future.

As he walked away the captain wondered if other crews had been as trying as this one? Or did he notice it more because he was now master of his ship? No. It was the mixture.

Submarines were still being heard, all within easy range. And soon after dark the convoy made another wide alteration of course. The captain saw they were going still farther south—he had among his papers the proposed mean line of advance.

Towards midnight a destroyer slid by the stern of the *Belgian Soldier*. The slender black silhouette of the racer was etched sharply against the risen moon, a silver wave curving high against the flare of her knife-like bow as she cut the water, her boiling wake leaving a straight line astern of her like a rod of white-hot steel. She sped away from the convoy. She had a distant purpose.

At sunrise a signal came from the commodore. "Avoid smoking." The master of No. 94 glanced at the funnel. A thin blue haze trailed from it. But he knew his ship had been as guilty as any of emitting volumes of black smoke at times, the tell-tale cloud which could be seen through good binoculars from the water's rim for twenty miles on a clear moonlight night like the one just past.

A corvette separated herself from guard duty and steamed out beyond the normal boundry to the north-west.

When the sun was approaching its zenith there reached the quiet bridge of the *Belgian Soldier* the sound of distant thunder, faint, yet there. Two rumbling peals. But there were no black clouds in the sky. Two hours later the missing destroyer and her consort came up from the starboard quarter and rejoined the convoy. One U-boat had been destroyed, leaving perhaps twenty more still free and threatening.

In the evening as the chief officer was walking aft he passed the curtained doorway of the chief engineer's cabin. There sounded to be some carousing within. Separating the curtains carefully to prevent the emission of light he stepped inside. The esteem which chief engineers were entitled to expect was not accorded the principal occupant when the chief officer spoke. He had no use for this drinking and the encouragement of others to do so. He harangued the chief for the periodic loss of steam. He blamed the engineers for this, not firemen who could be expected to swing the lead. The engineers on watch were too lazy to see that the coal was thrown in the furnace doors when the fires began to dwindle. He wanted to know whether the watertight doors in the stokehold bulkhead were shut at this moment.

There was some shilly-shallying about the question but when pressed the chief stated that the 'blackmen' had refused to shut them and he could not make them. If the captain still wanted them closed at night he had better give him the order in writing.

When this was related to the captain the latter saw no reason why he should transmit any such common sense order to the chief in this way. Next morning he spoke to him about it again.

That day, August 2, the eighth day out, the captain remarked on the thinness of the escort. The day before he had noticed that the destroyers were missing. He guessed that their high speed sorties had depleted their fuel and obliged them to make for Newfoundland before they ran out. For the second day and one night at least, as far as he could make out, there had been only four corvettes in the escort. How had the convoy escaped so long?

But at four o'clock in the afternoon, just after a scuffle on deck had been settled by the chief officer when some firemen had attacked the second cook for burning the bread, a group of six naval ships hove in sight. They took up positions in support of the well-tried mid-ocean group.

On the bridge of the *Belgian Soldier* the captain and third officer watched to starboard and astern as the perilous twilight descended. The sea was calm, the swell slight. The shadowy corvette abeam pitched a little. The warm southerly breeze was pleasant; and it was this wind that brought fog, but unfortunately not yet. Slowly it grew dark. The moon had not risen.

Then the convoy turned 45° to port, a manoeuvre that might elude but which set a course still more to the south, almost south-south-west, and they were already below the 46th parallel. Nevertheless it gave the commodore freedom to make a bold deviation to the west when he needed it.

The need came just after ten.

The captain had stayed where he was, the young officer occasionally moving about the bridge to gain a better perspective of the dark ship ahead by which he was steering.

A sound came across the water—the sound he had been waiting for, yet hoped he would never hear. A deep, muffled boom. Short, quick. That was all.

His heart, like the hearts of many, jumped. Before its beat quietened another detonation met his ears. Two red stars hung in the heavens somewhere to port—the rockets of distress. Then two more.

Suddenly the starboard side of the convoy was alight. Close to him, almost above him, large white flares fell from the dark sky. The *Belgian Soldier* and the ships ahead were revealed as though by searchlights. Then he saw that the edge of the convoy, ahead and astern and far to port, were also lit.

As if this were not enough, light flooded the very core of the massed ships as each vessel, including his own, sent up her pair of snowflakes. Suspended by small parachutes these torches revealed a fleet poised in perfect formation, like a still life impression, halted as though by shock.

This was the imprint fixed in his mind as the illumination went out; a sudden picture—and as quickly withdrawn. If the enemy was on the outskirts or within the columns surely he would be seen and guns brought to bear on him. That was the object. Beyond the convoy the escorts were now throwing up star shells, outwards towards the horizon.

When all light was gone and night, more intense in its blackness, fell upon the convoy once more, the commodore ordered his ships to wheel 90° to starboard in two turns of 45° separated by an interval of twenty minutes. The speed of advance was to be reduced to nine knots.

In slowing down still more, marking time as it were to allow the port wing to come round, the *Belgian Soldier* blew off steam—for once she was overburdened with pressure. The prolonged and penetrating shriek from the funnel was frightening.

When the safety valve closed the silence was profound until deafened ears had regained perception. It was then that the captain became aware of voices on the lower bridge and on the boat deck abreast the funnel; hurried demanding voices, loud, still unadjusted to the sudden quietness. He heard below him the clatter of oars being shifted.

He sent down to find out who was interfering with the boats. The third officer returned to inform him that many crew members were at the boats and a few in the big after boat on the port side. Although it was too dark to see for certain, from the voices he took them to be the chief steward and some of his staff.

By this time all the deck officers had congregated on the bridge but the station-keeping and the movement of the ship were still in the hands of the third officer, who was on watch, under the eye of the master. About twenty minutes after he had seen the ship ahead make the second turn and had told the quartermaster at the wheel to steer a course of 300°, he noticed that the ship he was following was going off to starboard again. It was so dark he had difficulty in seeing her but could do so with his glasses. He reported this to the captain who, looking through his binoculars, saw that the ship indeed bore away. He concluded that he must have mistaken the commodore's signal and that three 45° turns had been ordered rather than two. He told the officer-of-the-watch to follow her. The compass card finally settled on 345°. The ship was almost running north up the 47th meridian. The captain presently became rather surprised that he could no longer pick out No. 84, the rear ship of the next column. but he had No. 93 ahead of him.

Unfortunately No. 91, the leader of the ninth column, had made the mistake. A third turn was not the commodore's intention. She led the three ships astern of her away from the convoy at an angle of 45°. Their vulnerability increased with each turn of their engines.

The boat deck had quietened and all was silent on the bridge at eleven o'clock as the *Belgian Soldier* pursued her false course through the smooth sea.

At five minutes past eleven the fore deck suddenly opened. A thunderous roar split the calm air. The hull shuddered; the decks shook. The ship seemed to be pushed to one side, to totter to port. A pillar of water , as thick as a great tree trunk, rose before the bridge. Silver flecks of phosphorescence made it the more visible.

The column that hid the fore-mast broke like a fountain. It fell back dropping in a cloud-burst on the starboard side of the bridge. Water gushed in through the open forward windows of the wheel-house, through the door. Hunks of timber rained from above, ricochetted and went on down with the torrent. Strips of ragged tarpaulin thrashed against the woodwork, clung to stanchions. Then the sudden tide fell away spilling below and was caught by the scuppers.

The gigantic voice of the explosion lingered, drifted upwards and lost itself across the sea. The tumult of falling debris, as though coming to rest with sinister intent, ceased. The ship recovered her equilibrium, shook off the violent jar and plowed on into utter blackness.

His feet splashed on the wheel-house deck as the captain took two strides to the engine-room telegraph and rang 'stop'. There was no answering ring. He seized the handle again and swung it violently stopping it in the vertical position. Still no reply. He glanced at its face. It was invisible; the faint light inside the dial had gone out. Yet there should be a rung response. The voicepipe was shattered.

He heard the quartermaster reporting the light out in the binnacle; he had nothing to steer by.

The captain demanded a flashlight but none could be found. He looked down on the fore deck through the open window but in the darkness could only imagine a gaping hole. He ordered an SOS to be sent and heard someone shout the message to the radio operator. When he told the second officer to give the operator the ship's position the officer found that the chart-room door was jammed shut.

They fired the distress rocket in the port bridge-wing. The rocket apparatus on the starboard side was smashed and mangled with broken timber lying against it.

The general alarm did not sound when the button was pressed. But there was no one in the crew's quarters for the raucous bells to rouse; they were already assembled on the boat deck. In fact, some were about to abandon the ship.

In the darkness of his radio office the operator ran his fingers across the familiar panel. It was lifeless. The power to energize it could not be awakened.

He groped his way around the room until he found the small auxiliary set. As the panel warmed to the flow of current from the batteries he tapped out several times the slim message, 'No. 94 torpedoed,' which was probably enough.

He listened. His call of distress was answered. But he could not say where the *Belgian Soldier* was. At last he took the earphones off his head and by the little lights that blinked from the transmitter he found the handle of the door.

The luxury of shoveling coal through the open doors of the bulkhead that night ended abruptly for the three firemen in the stokehold. They were lifted off the plates, thrown, jarred. Coal shot through the watertight doorways. But the sound of coal being blasted out was obliterated by the eruption somewhere on the other side of the bulkhead.

The furnace doors had been thrown open—one had slammed shut again. Mercifully the live coals had not come out. As an added blessing the red glow from within provided light enough for the men to find the iron ladder that led them trembling, hardly able to grasp the rungs, up the black shaft to the cold air of the night above.

No such glow helped the fourth engineer in the engine-room. Utter darkness descended. The explosion might have been inside his submerged rectangular compartment. He slipped on the oily platform as the ship was thrust sideways but regained his feet. He followed the handrail he had grasped and reached the table where the logbook was kept. He knew there was a flashlight there. In a matter of seconds he had it.

The telegraph was ringing. He did not answer it. He made for the ladder; he could see it now.

The engineer might have had all the light he wanted had he stopped at the dynamo or the main switch-board. The ship would perhaps have been relit. But who was to know since it was not tried.

Once through the door at the top the fourth engineer ran along the steel deck and up to the boats. The donkeyman, who had been with him and had come up the same way when he got his bearings, followed him to the boats.

Seven or eight minutes after the torpedo had struck the captain and chief officer left the bridge. The quarter-master, gunner and lookoutman followed. The other deck officers had already gone down.

Those descending from the bridge found the rest of the ship's company, as far as they could make out in the darkness, occupying the two boats on the port side. Some were standing, some sitting on the thwarts. There was shouting and several sharp arguments were going on. A few climbed out and then got back. The boats were ready for lowering. But no order had been given to man them, much less abandon ship.

Having found the situation thus the captain accepted it. In fact, the forward boat of the two was about to be lowered and he himself lent a hand to ensure that the rope falls were kept clear for running. There were twelve men in the boat. He did not inquire if there was an able seaman in charge.

The lifeboat went down fairly fast and evenly. On striking the water it instantly veered away from the ship's side. Shrieks came from below, unintelligible yells.

The tiller had been toggled so that the rudder would direct the boat away from the danger of clinging to the ship's side. But the *Belgian Soldier* had more way on her than was expected. The falls could not be slackened enough to unhook the blocks as the boat sheered off. As it tilted the occupants moved to the high side. But the strain was too great and the boat capsized. It righted itself and remained afloat on its buoyancy tanks. It was dragged, swamped, alongside. Six men hung on; six did not. Their cries as they drifted away dwindled into the night. The six who held on climbed the ropes to the upper deck.

The after boat was larger and could accommodate fifty-two men. So it was not overloaded by the thirty-three who had elected to take possession of it. Included among these were the chief engineer, and the fourth engineer who had come up from the engine-room so hurriedly, the chief steward and his assistant and the two cooks. There were black faces and white and several languages used.

Though some were silent most were not. Terror-stricken shouts rose above the hubbub. There were probably none who knew what had happened to their shipmates in the other boat—they could not see and, because of the clamour, it would have been difficult to hear beyond the gunwale of their own boat. No one had assumed overall charge, not even the chief engineer—no deck officer was in the boat—but a number were demanding that it be lowered. Yet there was sensible communication between the two able seamen at the davits as they commenced to let the falls slip cautiously around the cleats.

About half way down the boat was fouled by a pilot ladder and began to tip but the ladder was cut away and the boat's downward progress resumed. It was virtually impossible for either of the seamen above to observe the trim of the boat—whether it was descending on an even keel or not. They could only hope that each was allowing the same amount of rope to run out. The chief officer was trying to estimate it, assess the misleading shouts from below, and pass the word to the seamen. They stopped with the boat just clear of the water, perhaps three feet. Then they went on warily.

The bow touched the water first and its rope allowed to run. But not being water-borne aft the bow dived, submerged, half rose and released the block. The whole boat filled and slewed around. All hands were thrown out, or washed out. The boat was dragged, waterlogged, stern first, by the after fall which did not unhook.

Eighteen men were borne away. On the cold waters of the Grand Banks the moving ship left them riding in their life-jackets, their little red lights, the few who had them, lighting automatically, making their slowly receding cries of despair the more desolate.

Fifteen clung on.

The chief officer, holding onto a davit, leaned out over the invisible water transfixed. Then he ran farther back and cut a small raft adrift.

To the captain who observed the tragedy the retreating voices sounded like the lament of a thousand souls—as though the spirits of all the seamen he had ever known were drifting out on an ebbing stream that would never flow again. If only he could reach them...

The panic that had driven so many into the boats now seized most of the few who had chosen to stay on deck. It spread to the officers who, except for the chief officer, had shown no leadership or exercised any authority. Some ran back from the bulwark. Several on the boat deck rushed to the remaining boats. Yet two or three helped those who had held on to the swamped boat to climb up the after fall one by one.

Thirteen succeeded in gaining the deck. It was a hard struggle for those weighed down by sodden clothes, easier for the lightly clad firemen. Two could not make it; they did not have the strength or else the skill.

The captain turned back to tell the men who had gone to the starboard boats to leave them and go to the rafts. The forward boat had been practically demolished; the after one, though not so visibly damaged, was holed.

Disregarding the captain, two men lowered the after boat. There was no one in it. When it reached the water it apparently sank to its gunwales and remained hugging the side of the ship, still hooked on.

Roughly twenty minutes had elapsed since the *Belgian Soldier* had been struck and fallen out of the wandering ninth column. She was down by the bow and had a slight list to port. Twenty-six men were in the water; twenty-seven remained of whom two were still in the big boat dragging alongside.

All those on board gathered on the after deck. The chief officer released the slip that held the big starboard raft to the main shrouds. With a rattle it slid down and shot over the side, its small white light automatically going on. The port one was launched at the same time.

The second engineer answered the captain's question at this time about the engine-room. It had, he asserted, partly flooded and some steam was about, water entering from the stokehold, he supposed; steam from somewhere. He maintained it was impossible to go down—otherwise the fourth and the donkeyman would not have come up so fast.

Though the captain knew he could not put much reliance on what the second said he asked him if the steam to the main engines had been shut off. The other assured him it must have been.

If the special cut-off valve on deck, which was there as an alternative in just such an emergency, had been working the captain could have been certain: but it was not working.

To his surprise, and obviously to the agonized distress of the others on deck, the captain saw that the starboard raft was being towed by its painter too far out from the side for anyone to reach. The large port raft had done the same thing.

Seeing this all hands left the after deck and went hastily forward.

Neither the captain nor any of the officers had been on the fore deck before. A survey of the disaster had not been carried out. The captain now took the opportunity to examine at deck level the extent of the damage.

Though he did not have a flash-light—he had never been able to find one—he could discern in the darkness a deeper blackness within the combing of No. 3 hatch. He stumbled against split and broken wooden hatch covers seemingly littering the deck abaft the foremast. He found himself treading on lumps of coal and sand ballast. He could not see whether the deck was buckled; it did not feel as though it was. The torpedo must have pierced the hull somewhere near the bulkhead separating Nos. 2 and 3 holds, probably just above the bilge.

The captain pressed on. Forward of the mast the deck was fairly clear of debris.

As the crowd gathered the bos'un slipped the gripe of the large raft in the starboard shrouds. It dropped with a reassuring splash. The two smaller ones were launched as added protection. Unlike the after rafts the big one stayed alongside and twenty men climbed down the rope ladder which had been dropped over and boarded it.

With so many on it it took to yawing about as it tilted first one way and then the other, and shook violently. The bos'un quickly realized that the cumbersome craft was being towed by the ship at a rate it was not built to withstand. He cut the painter and it became at once inert and sluggish in its overloaded state.

As the *Belgian Soldier* plowed on the raft bumped against the moving side. Men stood up to fend it off. Suddenly the waterlogged boat, which had been lowered by the two unheeding men and had been left to drag, appeared wallowing its way towards them. Fortunately they pushed the raft off enough so that it was struck by the boat's off-bow. The raft canted and swivelled but did not foul the boat. Then it closed with the ship's side again.

The struggles of the men to push it off had little effect. Nor was the attempt to propel it with its paddles any more successful. The raft continued to scrape along the hull and merely bounced off once or twice. Then it tangled with the big after raft which was still in tow but had lain too far off for the men to reach. It still hung clear of the side. There was considerable cracking of timber as the loaded raft jarred and twisted against the empty captive one but it squeezed through the gap.

They had only to clear the quarter now. But the raft persisted in clinging to the passing side. As the plating tended to slope inward under the counter the sailors' arms became too short to fend off. Moreover, the tipped-up stern caused by the flooding forward made her profile slimmer still. Even paddling could not counteract the hull's grasp.

The sound which now met their ears was unexpected. To all it was terrifying. The thrash of the propeller! The thrash of a screw half out of the water!

There was shouting; warnings to keep clear.

In a rain of silver drops the massive blades swung down and hit the water like a pile driver. Each blade as it came around was lighted by the constant luminescent shower. The propeller was approaching so fast there was little time to think of a way of escape. Yet some on the outside jumped into the water.

As it pounded past one black blade cut the raft in two.

When the parts floated clear no one was on either.

Several red lights bobbed about in the choppy wake as the din of the beating propeller diminished and was lost to sight. The raft's small white light still glowed on one of the halves.

Seven men climbed back or, floating, hung onto the lighted one, nine found the other part. Four could not reach either and drifted away. They may have been hurt by the blade.

The large raft on the port side of the fore rigging was launched soon after the starboard one had started its journey. On becoming water-borne it rocked and strained to its securing line as the other had done and it was difficult to board. Six went down the rope ladder, including the captain. As they cast off, which they realized they must quickly, another man jumped from the deck and was hauled aboard. He was thought to be the last of the crew to leave the stricken ship.

The captain recognized at once that the ship was moving faster than he could have believed. He had assumed that by this time, about half an hour after she had been hit and having no power, her way through the water would have been negligible. But he saw now she must be travelling at all of four knots.

The raft floated freely but hugged the hull. They could not push off.

Alarm gripped the captain. The boats!

They encountered the first in what seemed only a moment. The collision was severe and the raft jammed awkwardly between the boat's bow and the ship's side. It looked as though the boat would force the raft under its keel but its buoyancy prevailed and providentially it extricated itself and swung away.

The big boat came upon them with equal force. It was still being dragged stern first. The raft heeled, then pivoted and was thrown aside. As it freed itself they saw two men in the boat. The men called but their moment had passed. The raft cleared the boat too fast for them to jump. It came back against the ship again.

The large after raft swept by without touching them; it was being towed too far off. They merely had to avoid the taut painter.

As soon as the fuss of its wash subsided a throb became starkly audible, the familiar pulse and plunge of a propeller driving a light ship. The petrifying sound intensified with each revolution. It was at the end of the steel wall against which they were being jostled and which was now receding into the counter.

As the ship came on the screw was seen against a backdrop of white water thrown up by the emerging blades. The captain held his breath. Would they be picked up and thrown through the aperture? With a noise like a sucking pump, and hammer blows on the other side, the propeller came into them. The blade that was timed to hit them came up directly beneath and threw the raft out and flung it over.

But it did not break it.

All seven occupants struggled in the turbulent sea. One by one they regained the capsized raft.

Holding on to a life line before reboarding the captain saw the high dark stern of the *Belgian Soldier*, listing slightly, plowing on into the night, her rudder amidships, her screw turning as though some phantom watch was still in the stokehold firing the boilers. Water could not have reached the furnaces or risen high in the engine room.

A half moon came up over the horizon sometime after midnight. Under its light as it rose in the clear night sky each survivor who had not already perished in the cold water found himself in a small arena of desolation. Most were alone in their life-jackets, some with the small comfort of a red light floating beside them at the end of a lanyard.

The two halves of the broken raft still supported several men. The bos'un lay unconscious and two others were little better, each having been hit by the propeller blade.

The captain's raft had been paddled a considerable distance. The red lights had directed them and they had picked up four men. Faint cries were heard from time to time but those without lights could not be found. Several white flickering lights from the smaller rafts were seen.

About two o'clock those who were capable of observation, discerned the dark form of a ship gliding slowly across the moon's path.

Men shouted, though their shouts would not have been heard. The captain watched her intently. She turned, moved towards some lights on the water. There, at a little distance, she remained for a while. Then she manoeuvred to others and at length to the raft that had been the last to leave the ship.

A corvette of the support force that had joined the beleaguered convoy, HMCS *Galt*, had been detached to find the missing ninth column. Coming upon the lights scattered narrowly along a path of the sea, though not the ship which had travelled it, she picked up all the survivors she could find. She remained in the vulnerable area, stopped at times much to her own risk, until fog descended.

She rescued thirty-three men. A number had been taken singly from the water, several clinging to flotsam, one already dead. All those on the rafts were brought on board. Two of the injured on the broken raft were in a coma when lifted to the deck and died that night. The bos'un was alive but expired before dawn. The four were committed to the deep with the last rites in the morning.

Apart from the four who died after rescue, seventeen of a company of fifty-three drowned or perished from exposure, among them all the catering staff, the chief engineer and the fourth engineer who had left the engines running.

The ship herself had steamed on through the moon-lit fog, unsteered, unmanned, as though still trying to fulfill her purpose alone. No one knows how far she went. She stopped when her steam was exhausted and at some time went to the bottom, her short and valuable life ended.

The Music of the Wreck

Two surprising things happened that summer. Curiously enough they were both sequels of the same event, an event which had occurred more than forty years before.

In the first place, two keys on the Skinner piano, which had hitherto been silent, came to life. It was the First of July and everyone along the shore was there at the Odd Fellows Hall to wind up the holiday in traditional style; people from Beaver River and even from as far away as Bear Cove. The hub of the district had always been Port Maitland.

Captain Morton Skinner sat close to his piano. He had just heard the first of the new notes strike. It was a bass note but he did not know the name of it. When the significance of the phenomenon fully bore in upon him he immediately struck the closing bars of the dance. The hall ceased to shake and clapping replaced the thumping of feet.

His head a little on one side, his eyes shining yet quizzical, Captain Skinner repeatedly struck the key with his gnarled forefinger. The light from the candles in their ornate brackets on the blackened panelling of the upright shone on the silver in his hair. Then he played a tune which had the same note in it, and in the process discovered the second one that had never sounded before; at least, not in his time.

The captain, raising his spare frame from the stool, lifted the lid of the piano and looked at the mechanism inside, much as he would the engine of his boat when it coughed too much. Then with a smile on his lips he sat down and played the Squid Jigging Song again.

It must, he speculated, have been the uncommonly dry weather that had brought about the widened range of the piano. He was particularly glad now that he had personally supervised its transportation from his home to the Odd Fellows Hall up the road. It had been hauled on a dray by a yoke of oxen, as it had been every year that Captain Morton Skinner contributed himself and his instrument to the Dominion Day celebrations.

The other notable thing in the summer of 1958 occurred when young Hank Hopkins and his cohorts were engaged in picking blueberries in the patch between the Hopkins three-acre farm and the sea. Reconnoitring for a better fruit-bearing bush, Hank stubbed his toe on something that emitted a vague ring. On investigation he found that he had come in contact with the neck of a stone jar. With his blueberry-picking compatriots he dug with

Artist's depiction of the salvaging of the *Cobequid's* elegant piano by the skipper of the *Sadie.*

his hands in the sandy soil and extracted from the ground a five-gallon jar of dark liquid. When this was analyzed by the adults a search-party was organized, with Captain Skinner in the forefront. No fewer than five demijohns of rum were unearthed, their wicker casings withered to a dry bracken-like substance.

The discovery formed the basis of a celebration which was appropriately held aboard John Skinner's new vessel, he being the son of Captain Morton Skinner. It was attended, apart from the vessel's owner, by the several senior hands of the search-party, including Simon Welk. They started in mid-morning, and conjecture on who in the village of Port Maitland had originally buried the treasure gained impetus as the day wore on.

But its source was never doubted. All knew where the rum had come from, just as they all knew where Captain Skinner's piano had originally resided.

Forty-four years before, in February 1914, a blinding snowstorm struck the coast of Nova Scotia. The boats had been hauled up at Port Maitland— the lobster season did not open until March and few men fished in the deep winter months. As the blizzard thinned out in the early afternoon of the second day, two fishermen at the dock noticed a large steamer about six miles off, apparently heading up the Bay of Fundy. Then snow flurries hid her. Half an hour later fair visibility returned and the fishermen saw the ship again. They were surprised. She was in the same position, directly out across the turmoil of water from the little harbour.

"Something wrong," one said.

"Yea. Must be stopped. I'm going for my glass."

He picked his way up a trodden snow path to his house and presently came back with a spy-glass.

The big ship was quite clear in the circle of the lens. And there was no smoke blowing from the funnel, no wisp of steam. They took turns observing her through the telescope.

"Aground, I reckon."

"Fast aground," agreed the other.

They went over to the fish-packing office and told the man there he had better call Yarmouth.

The man spoke over the noisy telephone-line. "There's a ship off o' here and she looks like she's aground on Trinity Ledges."

The Royal Mail Steam Packet *Cobequid* had come up from the West Indies to Halifax in the middle of January and, after disembarking some of her passengers and discharging part of her cargo, started the short coastal voyage to Saint John, New Brunswick. She had just rounded Cape Sable when the snowstorm swept down upon her. She forged ahead, into the Bay of Fundy, through the thick grey-white atmosphere, stemming the fast-running ebb tide. Her master failed to see the Lurcher Light-vessel to windward, but hoped to sight Briar Island light ten miles farther up. Her progress was slower than appreciated and the north-west gale set her towards the Eastern Shore.

Shortly after midnight she struck. There was a sudden jolt; a shudder ran through the 5,000-ton ship as her bow drove onto a rocky ledge.

She sent out an SOS, the new signal of distress. Her message said that she was fast on Briar Island. A tug was dispatched from Yarmouth that night but could not find her. Dense though the snow was, the tug would have come upon the *Cobequid* had she, in fact, really been aground on Briar Island.

That night and the next day the passengers and crew of the liner waited; waited against the fury of the gale and the tide's prodigious rise and fall. Late in the evening the tug, sent this time to Trinity Ledges as a result of the telephone call from the wharf at Port Maitland, reached the ship. The weather was less tempestuous.

Morton Skinner was twenty-five when the *Cobequid* went aground. He had a major interest in a fishing-boat which he shared with Simon Welk. At five o'clock on the morning following the sighting of the wreck and the telephone call, Skinner and Welk slipped out between the breakwaters of Port Maitland in their thirty-two-foot *Sadie* (named after young Mrs. Skinner) well ahead of everyone else. During the previous windy afternoon, and until long after dark, the men at Port Maitland had been bringing their fish-boats down from the beach, having cleared them of snow and ice, and fuelled and started their engines. A wreck so close to home was not to be left to rust away now that the weather was turning fairer. But though the gale was abating it was still rough, and the *Sadie's* exhaust-pipe came out of the water frequently. Skinner took a circuitous route and came in from seaward towards the Trinity Ledges. With eyes accustomed to the night Skinner and Welk could see the stretch of white shoal water and hear it thundering over the Ledges. They could discern the ghostly black shape of the stranded liner. Skinner stopped the engine.

"We'll stay here a spell," he said, taking his hands off the small wheel in the pilot house and wrapping his arms round his tall, slim body. His mitted hands cracked against the back of his hard oilskin coat.

"Yea," Welk agreed. "Won't take long to find out if the hands are still aboard. No lights, anyway. But there's an almighty heavy sea running by her."

They dropped down to leeward silently. Now they could see the spindrift from the breaking sea flying high up the clearly etched hull. With the faint light of dawn they saw the large yellow funnel reaching up, and the high tapering masts.

"She can't take much more of that," Welk said. "She's sure going to break her back soon if it ain't broke already."

"If it stops blowing soon she'll likely hold together. But the tidal rise and fall will be hard on her."

Skinner had so judged the wind and distance that the boat drifted down to pass close under the broad-countered stern. They picked out the gold letters COBEQUID, and beneath her name the word LONDON. No figure was visible on her deck above, no hail came down from the poop.

Clearing the stern they had a view of the starboard side and there, abreast of the mainmast, was a long companion ladder reaching down to the water, the lower steps awash. Skinner and Welk were not to know that the last survivor had come down that companion just before midnight. Sixty passengers and the crew, which numbered about seventy, had been taken off by the tug only a few hours before. The twenty-year-old mail ship from England and the West Indies was in imminent danger of breaking up.

"We'll board her now, Simon, if you ain't agin' it," Skinner announced.

"I ain't agin' it, Mort," Welk answered, half indignantly. "That's what we come for. She looks like she's abandoned."

"Abandoned! Aye. But she wouldn't have been if she weren't going to split in two. Look at that sea alongside her."

Skinner kicked the flywheel and the combustion of the one-cylinder motor resounded against the tall heavy-plated side like an irregular deep-throated quick-firing gun. Welk threw a grapnel at the foot of the ladder as the boat tossed and wallowed. Cutting the motor Skinner leaped from the pitching craft. He caught the ladder. Welk, after waiting his chance, did the same. Up on deck all was silent except the sea below.

Skinner and Welk had opened No. 4 hatch and were in the lower hold before the others of the 'salvage' fleet joined them. Then the hatches forward were opened up; but the holds were flooded; they were exposed to the naked rocks beneath.

The first cargo they encountered in No. 4 was of puncheons. Their stencilled markings said 'Molasses.' All the hatch-covers had by then been removed to allow the daylight to penetrate.

"Say! Look ahere!" someone shouted from back in the hold. He came out into the square of the hatch with a demijohn.

"That's the goods!" said Welk.

"That's rum. Lets get her up on deck. We couldn't let one like that go to the bottom."

A fisherman near him said they weren't here for one of anything; they were going to get the lot up if they had time.

They were aware of another consignment of freight through their sense of smell. It permeated the whole of the lower hold. Sugar. It was probably down towards the bottom.

That day the derricks were raised, tackles rigged and cargo worked by twenty pairs of hands without the help of steam winches. As the weather improved, boats were loaded and taken in and discharged, probably at a faster rate than the cargo had been loaded in Barbados. By nightfall, when they had covered the hatches over, some of the men were making their third trip to shore. They were in a hurry. Who knew when her fateful hour would come? Moreover, there were the revenue men. They might appear at any moment.

The following day Skinner, who was mathematically inclined, counted upwards of a hundred men aboard the *Cobequid* hoisting out freight. They had come from the fishing-villages up and down the coast. And they were expert in the salvage of cargo; they needed no time-keepers or walking bosses.

Almost strangely they encountered no opposition in landing their salvage at the wharf at Port Maitland, and there was still less risk at villages like Cape St. Mary, seven miles farther up the Bay. This was mainly because Johnson, the customs officer, felt the matter to be beyond his jurisdiction. Johnson operated the local livery stable, and he was also the district mail carrier. In his levying work he knew all about the application of custom duty on salt coming up from the Indies for the fish-packers, but he was not sufficiently conversant with the customs act to be familiar with wreck-salvage. If he had had a fishing-boat he would have been out with the others. Until the government enquired into the action being taken by their representative in the person of Johnson, the coast was clear.

And even after a week of fine clear weather, which was unusual at that time of year, there had been no sign of the revenue men. Perhaps they were all engaged in more urgent matters.

"For sure the revenue guys must know what's aboard a vessel up from the South," Welk said, as he and Skinner were hauling a load of demijohns and molasses up from the wharf to their respective homes in one of the customs officer's smaller wagons.

"Oh, they have their troubles with them trading schooners, them as smuggles liquor in with their cargoes. Guess they're all taken up with prevention over to Halifax and Liverpool and Mulgrave, and don't know about this here ship. We'll see their cutter heave in sight soon enough, I dare say."

In the meantime the women of Port Maitland had already run into difficulties. The whole village encountered a warehousing problem. The two-storey frame dwellings were spacious enough but there were many children in them. These doubled up and the space made available was used for the storage of sugar, molasses and rum. But some of the women would not have liquor in their houses, not much anyway, twenty gallons or so to each perhaps. Most of it was kept outside. Some was buried.

On board the *Cobequid* interest had extended to other quarters of the ship, the holds having yielded by now an ample supply of perishables. The men found their way into the passenger quarters and store-rooms—auxiliary oil-lamps provided ample illumination to enter the deepest recesses of the commissariat. They had set up a system of destoring not unlike that adopted when a ship is being laid up by its owners for an indefinite period.

Soon villagers had linen sheets on their beds instead of flannel, and counterpanes emblazoned with the letters R.M.S.P. Towels with the legend Royal Mail woven across them hung in kitchens. Silver bearing coats-of-arms appeared on tables; and there was an extensive line in artistic china— even egg-cups had the interwoven initials in gold inscribed on their small curved surfaces. Indian rugs lay on the floors of parlours. The veterinary surgeon had some fine instruments the like of which even the visiting city doctor had never been seen to pull out of his bag. The natives were very pleased.

Then the revenue men swept into town; and they came by road, in a rig from Yarmouth. It took the villagers by surprise. However, fog set in with their arrival.

"Never so glad to see it come in thick, Mort," Welk told the skipper of the *Sadie* as they slipped out of the little harbour.

"Wouldn't trust them revenue men," Skinner snorted, not turning his head from the direction he was steering. "Could be a blind though, them fella's coming in by rig. Calculate the revenue cutter can find her way to Trinity as easy as we can." He spat to leeward.

It was with the appearance on the scene of this liquor law enforcement agency that Morton Skinner knew he must tackle his biggest and most formidable job at once. It was rather late in the great episode to undertake the task of removing such a cumbersome piece of furniture, because it was obvious that Johnson's disinterest in the broader aspects of his customs responsibilities would be reported to higher authority through the revenue men and the delinquency of the department rectified at last. Moreover, the weather had been extremely kind and could not last much longer—the comparative calmness of the Ledges could be turned into an unapproachable steaming cauldron at any moment.

But things were getting a bit out of hand on the *Cobequid.*

An adequate supply of rum had been laid out in the ornate green card-room at the head of the grand staircase overlooking the promenade deck. Workers refreshed themselves here on their trek up from the bowels of the ship and often on their way back from loading. It was on the main route. *Modus operandi* was discussed by fishermen sitting on needle-point chairs. Even cards were played. Skinner had revived himself in this happy place but he was more interested in the job which had so strongly commended itself to the more artistic side of his nature. For he had the piano on his mind, the one he had seen in the great saloon. He had tried the instrument and it had seemed wonderful to him.

He had somehow inherited a musical talent. When he was a boy he had been encouraged, and taught in a way, to play the pianoforte when he visited an aunt in Annapolis Royal at harvest-time and on other special occasions. After that he had always wanted to play. Now was his chance if he could acquire this beautiful upright piano.

But how to get it out of the ship? First it had to be unbolted from the deck; then it had to be taken up the grand staircase. He had enlisted men several times to help carry it, but on each occasion they had advocated going to the card-room to fortify themselves first. Even Simon Welk suffered lapses of this kind while searching for assistance. Finally, Skinner persuaded Simon's brother Willie to lend his great strength and he talked Willie Welk's partner Joe into it, too.

"All right, Mort," Joe ultimately agreed, "but it's a heck of an awkward machine to move."

However, they had all heard that Morton could play and they knew it was not idle acquisitiveness. So they went below and cut the securing bolts adrift with a saw, lit the candles on either side of the piano to improve the lighting on the way up and, with rope slings over their shoulders, hoisted the 600-pound instrument up two decks by way of the staircase.

It was a business getting it past the card-room door, but Skinner eventually achieved it by saying he had found a cache of cigars which he would distribute when the piano was safely in his boat. They wheeled it along the promenade deck on its casters, which was not difficult, although it had a tendency to run into the scuppers because of the starboard list. On the after deck they passed two slings round it and hoisted it on the end of a derrick over the side and down into the *Sadie*. In the boat Skinner and Simon Welk manoeuvred it in such a way that, as Willie Welk lowered it, it landed beautifully on its back across the gunwales in the after end. They lashed it down as best they could with the sling, and Joe threw down a coil of rope to help hoist it out when they reached the wharf. Then they all went up to the card-room.

It was dark and still foggy when they came out on deck, but they noticed that a southerly breeze had sprung up. With the tide running over the reef a disturbed sea was created, and Skinner and Welk saw that their boat was jumping about awkwardly and rubbing her wooden strakes against the steel hull. Moreover, the piano, lying across the boat like a plank on a pair of trestles, was taking the occasional bump. And the stern was uncomfortably low in the water.

"We'll put a coir fender on her, Simon," Skinner said, "and then we've got to put her into better trim. You jump down and I'll get something heavy."

The remaining men on board were leaving and they helped Skinner haul some bags of sugar to the rail.

"I'll lower you down some sugar, Simon," he shouted.

Simon Welk seemed unable to stow the cargo properly but perhaps it was because of the way Skinner lowered it. However, after four bags had gone on the wrong side of the gunwale and sunk, Welk landed two by the pilot-house door.

"Stow 'em in the fore end of the cabin," Skinner ordered.

"Can't do that, Mort. It's choc-a-block with them cushions you wanted."

"Well, put 'em on top of the house, close up in the bow."

But Welk fell over when he lifted one of the hundred-pound bags to the level of his chest. "She's pitching something terrible down here, Mort. Give us a hand."

"You just can't stand proper. You been imbibin'. Where's your sea-legs?"

They eventually loaded ten bags in the midship section and together restowed them up on the little deck above the pilot-house. With this distribution of ballast the piano aft was compensated for and the *Sadie* assumed an even keel, though she was quite low in the water.

Skinner turned the flywheel.

"Come on, let's get going."

Once they had lost the lee of the ship and cleared the Ledges they discovered the wind was stronger than they had thought. The tide was in full flood, which tended to make the waves longer and more even, but the *Sadie's* stability was not as positive as it should have been.

Skinner tried steering different courses to ease the rolling and found that nor'-nor'-east was about the best. Nevertheless, he and Welk decided to proceed slowly in this direction and then try south-east later on, and so work in by stages.

After half an hour it began to rain and soon it came down in torrents. This cleared some of the fog and flattened the sea a little, but it did not improve the visibility, which was one thing they were pleased about. Presently Skinner swung the wheel over to try the south-easterly course. As he came beam on to the sea the boat rolled severely and, with a horrible grinding sound, the piano slid away from the starboard gunwale. Skinner winced, but had to give his full attention to the boat to bring her up in the wind.

Simon Welk had been dozing just inside the pilot-house door, having been overcome by the soporific effect of the rich rum within him. But he was out and around the engine-box before Skinner's shout was drowned in the downpour.

"Hold it, Simon! Don't lose that piana." He was tending the wheel and easing the motor. Welk did not reply to the impossible instruction. But he could see that the piano was still there—though only just. It seemed to be teetering on the port gunwale. One lashing was still holding it back on the little transom deck.

An alarming list had developed and water was slopping in over the low side. And the stern seemed lower in the water, the bow up. Even her fore-and-aft trim seemed to be lost.

"Gee, Christmas! I don't like this," Skinner complained, looking round from his steering position. The little *Sadie* was not pitching properly; she rolled sickeningly.

"She's going to turn over or sink by the stern, Mort. Only way's to keep her into the eye of the wind."

"Take the wheel, Simon, and let me have a look."

They exchanged places and Skinner laid hold of the piano and bent all his strength to moving it inboard. He had about as much success as Mohammed had with his mountain. The boat lay over on her beam ends and ducked her stern under periodically.

After a particularly nasty lurch, when at least a ton of water came inboard, Skinner made up his mind about jettisoning the cargo.

"Hold on your wheel, Simon," he shouted. "I'm going to cut the lashing and let her go. Pass me that coil of rope that Joe threw down."

"What you going to do?"

"Buoy the piana. I ain't going to lose her."

"Water's too deep here for that length o'rope," Welk advised.

"Well, we'll try it."

Skinner made the long rope fast through the legs of the piano then cut the lashings. The next roll took it.

It was an ugly moment. The port gunwale was held under water and the engine stuttered. Then the vessel righted. The cargo was gone.

"Pay it out free," Welk shouted as Skinner tended the coil of rope as though it was a mooring line. He had secured the inner end to a ringbolt. Welk stopped the engine.

Presently the rope became taut. It took the weight nicely.

"She's not on the bottom," Welk asserted, "water's too deep." He felt the tension of the rope. "We could tow her, though, Mort."

Morton Skinner looked over the side. "That's right. That's right. Sure we could! Better than mooring her, anyway. Okay. We'll shift that sugar aft now, or heave it over the side. Then we'll get on to the pump. Water's washing around my knees aft here, pretty near."

They were vaguely conscious of the boat being on an even keel. When they got up on the pilot-house they knew why. Their ballast had more than half gone—the rain had had a remarkable effect on the sugar. That was why, they realized, the stern had become so low. They threw the sacking into the sea.

Progress was slow owing to the drogue at the end of the rope. While Skinner steered directly for Port Maitland, Welk stayed aft with his hand on the rope, which led out through a fair-lead. After twenty minutes he felt it slacken.

"She's hitting the bottom, Mort."

"That's the six-fathom shelf," Skinner announced, "only its eight fathoms at this stage of the tide. Piana's probably upside-down. Hope her guts don't get full of sand. We got to raise her up."

It was hard work; the piano was like a heavy anchor. But they lifted it off the bottom.

Having jogged along another half-mile the piano bounced again. After a long haul they got it up fairly short. Then they heard Port Maitland's bell-buoy through the heavy rain. Near the top of the flood they thought they could make the wharf without the piano touching again.

They berthed clumsily, because of the encumbrance under the stern, and when they were tied up Skinner said they would rest her nice and gentle on the bottom, like a lobster pot.

"No point in being gentle now, Mort."

"Oh, she ain't bashed up. Fact is, I'd like to sight her." He glanced along the dark, glistening fish-scaled wharf. "But I daresn't without surveying the neighbourhood."

They left plenty of slack on the rope so that it looked like an idle line hanging over the side. As they walked up the wharf in squelching boots Skinner said they'd get the piano up tomorrow, late probably, maybe after dark.

But the next day from early morning until late at night the wharf seemed to Welk and Skinner to be seething with activity. There were revenue men certainly, and Johnson, but he had two other customs officers in blue uniforms with him, and there were city men with hard hats and expensive overcoats. The rain had stopped but it was windy. Then a tug came in with a barge and took some of the people aboard and the craft went out again, obviously to the wreck. The salvage experts had arrived at last. After that there were always men at one end of the wharf or the other—marine-disaster types and government people. Laden barges were brought in and they filled the little harbour, and the fishermen were asked to keep their boats further up the wharf.

It was this request, a veiled demand—and the villagers did not wish to incur any displeasure by objecting—that gave Skinner the idea.

They worked around their boat in the latter part of the afternoon, and in the course of their tasks, when not under what they felt to be direct observation, they managed to hoist the piano clear of the bottom. Warping the boat round the end of the wharf and some distance up it on the other side they pushed off and anchored close in to the sloping shingle beach beyond the fish-packing plant. There they remained until after dark, at which time they shortened the piano-rope close up and worked the boat in as near as they could to shore. It was almost high water. Then they waded ashore and went up to Skinner's back yard.

With Willie Welk and Joe they lifted the Skinner privy clear of its pit and dismantled the seat. They carried the little shed down to the shore and set it up at the water's edge. Morton Skinner acquainted his wife with what he had done while the four men were working the spigot of a rum keg in the parlour waiting for the tide to fall. Sadie Skinner said she could accommodate herself.

At two a.m., the tide having fully receded, they all went down to the shore. Both boat and piano were high and dry, but it was very dark and things on the beach were not easily seen. They carried the piano up the shingle and placed in on its end in the privy and shut the door.

In the morning Johnson's dray and oxen were employed in hauling the privy up from the shore, past the revenue men, the customs officers and the hard-hatted salvage officials to Skinner's back yard close to his kitchen door.

That same day a great storm came up and the *Cobequid* broke up. But it was August before the piano had dried out and Captain Morton Skinner had worked on its tuning to the point where he could play his old favorite, the Squid Jigging Song.

At low water, during pronounced spring tides, you can still see the frames of the *Cobequid*, green with thick sea growth and barnacle-encrusted, just beneath the surface on the south side of Trinity Ledges. And if it is very calm and quiet when you go there, with the sun shining, you might imagine you can hear the tinkle of piano keys.

Bound
for
Rome

"And when neither sun nor stars in many days appeared, and no small tempest lay upon us, all hope that we should be saved was taken away."

Thus went an entry in a log of a grain ship transporting prisoners through the Mediterranean. It was written by a passenger. The log survived not only that tempestuous voyage but weathered the high winds and doldrums that beset Christendom for two thousand years thereafter. The passenger was Lucanus, a Syrian from Antioch, the son of a freed slave, a physician and itinerant writer.

Myra basked in the clear air of the high Lycian coast. A mile or so below the September breeze ruffled the blue water of the harbour of Andriaca, Myra's port. As the company of legionaries, prisoners, and several independent passengers approached in the little Asian trader which had brought them on the first leg of their journey from Caesarea and Sidon, they saw, among the vessels lying inside the stone mole, a ship of striking proportions. The centurion Julius knew now that he would be able to transfer his captives to a vessel that would take them directly to Rome. But he had not expected to be so fortunate as to find one of the largest ships afloat waiting there in the harbour as though to meet them. She belonged to the great fleet of carriers employed in the Egyptian grain trade.

Moored bow and stern to anchors the Roman ship lay like a colossus on the water, her hull rising dull red for a full thirteen feet amidships to her yellow bulwarks. It was with a sense of reprieve from discomfort that the four most concerned, Julius, Paulus, Lucanus and Aristarchus, surveyed her as their small, cramped vessel anchored close by.

Lucanus, the most susceptible to aesthetic expression, spoke in measured praise of her lines, the strength of her heavy beams, bevelled where they projected through her sides below the deck, the thick fifty-foot mainmast surmounted by a tall topmast. He acclaimed the beauty of her sternpost which grew into an acrostole ascending in a graceful forward curve above the quarter-deck and curving again to a gilt swan's head whose bill rested on her throat. The bow rose in harmony and reached up and out to a prow resembling an arm and fist held high above the stem. Lucanus admired the broad blue band embracing her length which slimmed her bulky girth. The ripples on

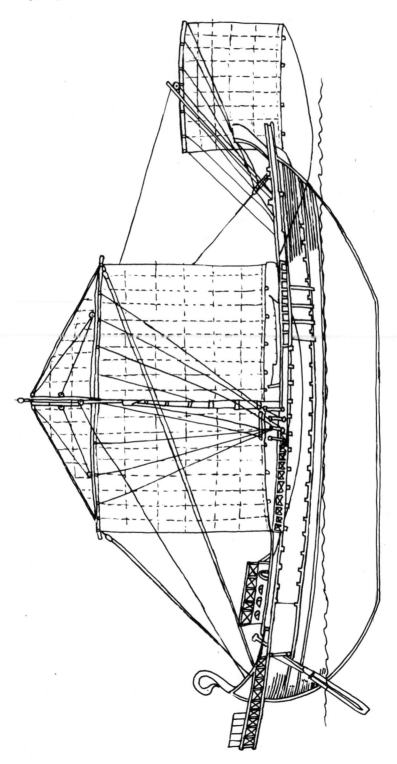

Roman Grain Ship

the water revealed now and then the Roman green of her under-body. As though to soften the combination of colours the prow and the swan's neck were painted white.

Paulus wakened on the grain ship next morning to the sound of singing, deep-throated and harmonious. Out on deck he found the seamen hauling in the dripping bower anchor cable to the rhythm of their song. The swell and fade of distant voices on the warm calm air of sunrise told of other vessels weighing anchor too.

A zephyr filled the red triangular topsails for a moment; then it hesitated and the sails fell slack. Presently a steadier current of air caught them. They tightened. As the land breeze from the hills and mountains beyond Myra increased, gratefully cooling, the heavy mainsail filled. The stern anchor was weighed and the men at the tillers steered for the gap in the mole.

There was no time to be lost in getting away. Navigation in the Great Sea would cease before long; it was the end of September. The uncertainties of wind and sea and the frequent absence of heavenly bodies would prevent it. She was the last ship of the grain fleet to leave the East bound for Puteoli in the Bay of Naples or the newer port of Ostia at the mouth of the Tiber before the winter set in.

But it did not seem treacherous on that peculiarly hot sun-filled day as the big ship cleared the mole and set a course in the light north-easterly wind through the deep channel between the cliffs of the mainland and a group of high islands. At midday, as they stood out to sea, the wind backed to the north, then to the north-west, the direction they wanted to pursue, though it did not blow strongly. It became a slow beat to windward.

Paulus and Aristarchus were still as much prisoners as those who had been in chains at Myra, now released and employed by the soldiers. Paulus and his Thessalonian friend, companion of his earlier travels, were being accorded a generous hospitality. The Roman Julius had insisted, and gained the captain's consent, that they share the cabin accommodation in the deck house with the several privileged passengers, including their close friend Lucanus. The centurion himself had a berth in the great-cabin. The captain had a small room there to himself.

Julius had been considerate from the beginning. In fact, he had had their fetters unshackled as soon as they had sailed out of Caesarea. A centurion of the renowned Augustan Cohort, the emperor's own regiment, Julius was the escort of a man of fame (though infamous in the eyes of the Jews) to the heart of justice, the highest tribunal in the Roman Empire.

By evening it was calm. But the following day the contrary wind from the north-west returned, the etesian wind from the mountains of Macedonia which was drawn across the sea by the heat of Arabia into Egypt and Palestine. And again at sunset it fell calm and the ship lay almost still in the low swell, the sails limp at the slowly swinging mainmast.

At dark a lantern was lighted beneath the painted awning of the captain's balcony which overhung the stern and a small group from the great-cabin sat about on stools. Paulus spoke with elation of their changed circumstances.

The captain, a small white-haired man, passed some uncomplimentary remarks about the *Navis Rotunda* from which they had transferred. The pregnant coaster, as he called her, was almost half as fat as she was long. He was asked the length of his own ship and he gave her dimensions as 130 feet in length on deck with a thirty-seven-foot beam, widening to thirty-nine feet at the waterline. She could carry 20,000 talents; thus she was 500 tons burthen.

Paulus explained to the captain that the reason for their enjoyment of their freedom of movement was mainly because he and Aristarchus had been in prison in Caesarea for more than two years. "But that was a good thing really," he added, "because we would probably have been killed by the Jews if we had been free."

"But you are a Jew, are you not?" the captain asked. Paulus's cultured voice, his facial characteristics, scarred though they were from stonings and ill-treatment, portrayed that of a high-born Jew, yet his physical form was odd: broad and squat with short crooked legs. Nonetheless, he had dignity of bearing.

The lantern above them swayed gently, its light-beams gliding slowly back and forth across the wide deck planking.

"I am a Jew; once a Pharisee, trained as a rabbi; yet a free-born Roman of Tarsus, a great city of scholars, the caravan crossroads of the East. As you know," he said, as though to emphasize his acquisition, "the emperors bestowed the citizenship of Rome upon its wealthier inhabitants. I am as familiar with Roman thought as Jewish. I speak, as you hear, like a native Greek. I am a Christian—became so of a sudden long ago on the road to Damascus. Then I became a preacher and wandered through many countries. The response was great at times, little at others. I failed often." He grinned. "I am a captive too—but in more ways than you see me now."

The captain, much older than Paulus, probably well over sixty, looked with even greater interest at the sturdy little man whose black eyebrows met on the bridge of his slightly hooked nose. "In what other way?" he asked kindly.

Paulus shifted on his stool as though his limbs were cramped. "I was captivated by a Man who was once crucified, yet lived. He has meant...everything to me. And I am anxious to see Him again."

"I do not understand you."

"You will before the voyage is over."

"You are going to meet Caesar." The captain frowned as he saw no other more important person.

"Yes. At my own request; which, of course, cannot be denied a Roman citizen-prisoner. I have wanted to go to Rome for years. I was once 'told' that I would. That is why I demanded to be tried before Caesar. But I could wish the emperor were someone other than the youth Nero."

"Tried for what!" It was Julius who suddenly broke in. "That is the question I have asked myself; and would have asked the Judean governor Festus, or even Herod Agrippa, if I had not been your warden in the audience-chamber. Had I been a tribune it would have been different. But the ear of the proconsul, still less that of the king, would not have heard the questionings of a rough soldier. They did listen to you."

"But to no advantage to themselves unfortunately. And I think they really knew, as you do, my dear Julius, the falseness of the charges brought against me by the Jews of Jerusalem. But all things work for the best for those who speak the truth."

As the days advanced the etesian wind became stronger, the sea rougher. After continually beating against it they at last weathered Rhodes and struggled on up the rugged Ionian coast.

Though the ship was large and comfortable. by comparison with others her relatively narrower-gutted hull lay deep in the water and she was wet as she punched into the sea. It had been pleasant at the beginning when the throng on deck stood about in the sun or squatted in the shade of the mainsail; lay under the stars in the dewy nights. Now the poorer passengers and thinly clad prisoners felt the chill of the wind and the cut of salt water flung over them in showers. But the legionaries accepted it; they seemed content with their thoughts of returning home after service in the garrisons of Palestine. The crew, of which there were many, were used to it.

The captain's purpose was to sail as far into the Aegean Sea as would permit him to go about and pass close under the Greek peninsulas and so up into the Sea of Adria, thence to the Strait of Messina. But progress was slow and hard and the ship laboured; these winds of summer were outlasting their season.

It was nearing the ides of October when they came in sight of Cnidus, its houses shining white in the autumn sun on the isthmus behind precipitous Cape Krio. They could go no further.

"I cannot go on," the captain told the centurion. "We are too late."

He turned his ship and ran her on a broad reach a hundred miles to Crete. But off Cape Salmone the wind was still contrary so that he had to skirt the eastern end of the island hoping for fairer winds on the south coast.

Paulus felt the relief of being in the lee of the land for half a day, free from the rise and fall of the ship. But they soon turned into the wind again as they attempted to make progress to the west. The weather was no better. A long beat once more. Several days passed as they strove against it.

"The ship sails well close-hauled," the captain told Julius when he asked about their speed of advance. "Almost seven points into the wind," he said admiringly of his ship. "A performance few vessels can equal: few can tack at all. As for advancing westward, it is slow, very slow... But we are making the passage," he added laconically.

It was a case of standing out to sea and then heading partially backwards into the land, picking up only a little ground on each tack. And although the south coast of Crete offered shelter from the rough north-westerlies, sudden and violent off-shore cross squalls descended from the central mountain range and beset the vessel.

At length, after making good a distance of eighty miles along the coast, they came up under Cape Littinos, a headland they had had in sight all day, and worked into the harbour of Fair Havens. There they dropped anchor a mile from the town of Lasea.

The harbour—rather more a roadstead—was not as fair as its name; there were no anchorages along the south coast of Crete that could be called safe for big ships in autumn and winter; no experienced master could feel confident that his anchors would hold in the gusts of wind that came down the ravines. The water deepened rapidly at Fair Havens as it shelved away in conformity with the steep foreshore so that if the anchors dragged over the rock and gravel bottom they were soon out of their depth and the ship loosed to the elements. Moreover, the harbour was protected only from the west and north. Two small islands gave some shelter to the anchorage against the easterly winds that would come but it would not be enough. However, they were fortunate to have made the roadstead and lie comfortably enough for a while so that they could observe the weather and consider what they should do.

The crew, who numbered nearly a hundred men—needed more for the task of loading and discharging cargo than for sailing the ship—were immediately employed in over-hauling the running gear: splicing new parts into chafed ropes, replacing blocks and tackles here and there, setting up the shrouds and massive backstay. An officer took the boat away with empty casks to replenish the water supply at one of the streams nearby which had become a torrent from the hard showers. Eight men pulled it with the precision of long practice.

Lucanus, following his profession, moved among the crew and passengers attending their physical ailments, which were fewer than in most ships half the size, particularly galleys, with which Lucanus was quite familiar, where sores and disease abounded.

The captain spoke with gratitude for this to Paulus. "I seldom have a doctor travelling in my ship and this friend of yours is an able physician." He gazed at the deck and then out to sea as though searching his mind. He started to speak, hesitated, then looked at Paulus who was standing as solidly on the deck as a mooring post. "I have heard that you can heal men, too," he remarked at last. "Your brother Lucanus does so by virtue of his skill and learning, his instruments and herbs. You are not a physician as he is. Is it true that you can cure people without these things?"

Paulus watched two seamen placing a new strip of leather beneath a brail of a sail. Knowing the kindred trade of tent-making he had a natural interest. "I am a preacher," he answered slowly, "not a healer—of the body at least—though I have been granted the power to heal a few in an emergency or where I could see faith residing in the heart of a sick person."

"I am glad to hear it. Sickness and plague are curses when you have them among seamen. I may need you both before the end of the voyage. We will want all the health we can keep for what may be ahead of us. I do not like this place. Even now, if we have a hot day, the insect can carry malaria from the swamps of the river mouths."

Paulus looked at him sharply. "I know malaria. It stabs like a red hot needle driven into the temple and leaves you unnaturally sweating: and is embarrassing when you have urgent tasks to do. It can overtake you on the road where you have no shelter to lay your head; and I suppose it can render a man useless at sea."

"It can," answered the captain and gave his attention to the boat returning with water.

When the casks were taken on board he instructed the storekeeper to go in the boat to Lasea and see what fresh food he could buy. He gave the officer at the steering oar orders to watch the wind. "If it comes from the east or south return at once." The captain watched the boat until it disappeared around the mole extending out from the waterfront of the little town.

After several days of waiting during which the wind hung between west and north, the sky mostly cloudy and rain falling in heavy showers periodically, making it disagreeable for everyone on the open deck, Julius, who had talked to the captain often, called a meeting in the great-cabin. He invited Paulus and his friends, all of whom were widely travelled. The ship's officers also attended.

"The question is," the centurion announced, "are we to resume the voyage when a fair wind blows or stay here?"

The centurion being the senior personage on board, holding final authority, had to make a decision. And the time had been reached when the danger of going on might be greater than the danger of remaining under the uncertain protection of the cliffs of Crete.

The captain was unwilling to stay much longer. The hazardous season for navigation was already well advanced and he emphasized that when that period was passed they would enter the months when no ship would risk the sea at all. "When it comes fair it may blow too hard. It would be better to go now," he said, spreading his hands in exhortation, "while we still have the north-westerlies, and run for Alexandria and stay there until the spring."

"No, no, you cannot do that, Captain," Julius protested. "Not with my prisoners. That would be equivalent to going back whence we came."

"This is a summer roadstead. I cannot winter here." The captain spoke as master of his ship. "It is too exposed. The partial shelter of those two islands in a winter wind is not enough. We could be on the rocks to leeward if a gale from the east blew hard; and we could drag out to sea in a northern blast. Besides, the town of Lasea is too insignificant for the enjoyment of my crew—or your soldiers. And the ship is too crowded for exercise. Remember, we have upwards of three hundred men on board."

"We should review again the wisdom of going on to Phoenix which is supposed to be more protected for wintering," Julius declared. "You and your officers have agreed that it is a fairly secure harbour."

The centurion looked around at those assembled before him. Sunlight coming through the starboard windows of the great-cabin and through the arched doorway where the curtain had been drawn back, fell in shafts across the deck. A sunbeam resting on the white linen tunic of an officer put into duller contrast the long brown garments of the Nazarenes. An inexpensive jewel defending the Roman from the evil eye sparkled from an armband. Paulus spoke.

"It is not wise, in my opinion, to venture abroad now. The Day of Atonement—our Fast; your autumnal equinox—is more than a month gone. As the captain says we are in the dangerous period. Well before we could reach Sicily, if we made the attempt, we would be overtaken by winter weather when it is well known that ships do not venture into open water. There is not a sail at sea even now as far as we have seen. I know the dangers," he stressed with conviction. "I have been adrift before. Three times I have been shipwrecked." He gestured with his hands while his dark eyes covered his audience as they had done years ago when there were many to listen to him. "I can see, my dear friends, that should you leave here the voyage will be disastrous: it will mean grave loss; loss not only of the ship and the cargo but also of life. This is not foretold to me; it is my own opinion. For myself I do not care: I have run the great race. Nonetheless, I strongly advise against departure."

Lucanus and Aristarchus agreed with Paulus but the officers sided with the captain. While the majority was in favour of leaving the treacherous roadstead Julius refused to allow the captain to turn back. This made the little captain angry and he said he wished he had cleared Myra before the centurion had arrived with his useless minions. Had it not been for the late harvest in Egypt he would have been in the Bay of Naples well before this.

"Do not speak of my soldiers with disrespect," Julius thundered. "Your life and liberty are dependent on our legions."

"Stop this argument," Paulus directed, holding up his hand.

The captain winced. Lucanus smiled. The centurion started again.

"I am not forcing you to go on to Rome," he said, genuine good will evident in his deep voice, "I am advocating that we sail at the first opportunity for Phoenix. The harbour is only forty miles up the coast. And there by the gods we can stay."

"By what gods?" Paulus enquired quickly. "There is only one...But never mind. You have a majority, Julius, so let us have no further discussion."

Thus the meeting was concluded and the monotonous routine resumed.

The sixth day's dawn was different. The sun came up in splendour along the edge of the eastern shore, its long path scintillating down the placid, pale blue sea of early morning. Paulus watched it with his recurring wonderment of nature and nature's god as he stood on the gallery at the stern of the Roman merchantman. The glistening rays, glancing from the damp cliffs of Crete, stabbed his weak eyes and made him look away to wisps of mist suspended over a river mouth. Was summer here again? Had his belief in winter's approach been false?

When the sun had risen to the height of the mountain range a south wind ruffled the water. At once the ship became alive: the rattle of blocks as tackles were cleared, shouts from aloft, the splash of water thrown to the deck from buckets and the rhythmic hiss as it was swept into the scuppers.

A song drifted away on the warm, gentle wind as the anchors were weighed. The quarter rudders were lowered, their slim tillers manned, and the artemon was set below the overhanging foremast to aid the steering; the red topsails were hoisted and, as the light breeze held, the big emblazoned mainsail was unfurled from the yard.

The ship worked out slowly, rounded the headland and swung to the west-north-west for Phoenix which lay, with good luck, a day and a half's journey beyond.

In spite of his misgivings Paulus was delighted to be away again. The faint rustle of the wake was an attractive sound as the great grain ship moved sedately through the tranquil sea, her boat, which they had not waited to take in, tugging at a rope astern. Beyond the gracefully arched neck and gilded head of the swan Paulus saw the helmsman on the cabin house at the starboard rudder moving his tiller lightly while watching a distant point of land and now and then the fullness of the mainsail.

In the hush of the morning Paulus' thoughts turned momentarily to himself. He wondered why he had been so quiescent; why he was not more dynamic now, more forceful and exuberant in his speech; in fact, not passionately declaiming the precepts by which he had lived so long. Perhaps there was not the need here. Yet where was the firey character, where the orator, the persuader, the man of love who won the heathen—slave or rich— and withstood the rejection and the persecution of his opponents. Why? Paulus answered it simply. On the ship he was at peace; he was resting as his years demanded. Not many men lived beyond two score and ten. Few could have survived what he had; the scourgings, the lash, the stonings, starvation and imprisonment. He had striven against controversy and misrepresentation. Yet despite these vicissitudes was his spirit not the same? No doubt if the need came again he would be as vocal and vigorous as before. In Rome and to the limit of the West, if the pleasure of the emperor allowed him, he would teach with unflagging zeal.

He would like to have written to his friends in Philippi and in Ephesus but he had no scribe here, though he knew Lucanus would serve. But he could not impose such a tedious task on him. His letters must wait. In the meantime he would rest his mind and his body while the ship permitted it.

The captain kept close to the land and by careful observation estimated the speed to be a little over one knot. The coastal fringe was high with here and there a deep valley splashed with green which they gradually came up to and, step by step, left behind. Gladness seemed to pervade the ship. And a quiet night followed a day of peaceful sailing, the first since leaving Myra.

At daylight the point around which Phoenix lay was seen ahead against a clear hard horizon. But the dawn brilliance of the day before was nowhere; the glory of the sun was succeeded by a dullness that was ominous; a stratum of grey cloud encased the sky. Not unexpectedly, though tragically, the south wind presently failed and the sails slatted. The heavily laden vessel lost way.

Then an offshore catspaw was seen shivering the water. Soon its ripples overfell. Then, with the suddenness of thunder, a gust of wind came down from Crete's barren stony wastes and caught the ship aback.

The captain's voice could be heard above the squall as the seamen strove to seize the changed wind. With straining muscles the main brace was hauled alee and the long yard swung over. Capturing it, the great hull heeled to the starboard tack. The little captain now tried to claw his way to windward and close the shore.

The struggle went on while the wind hauled and increased until it blew with such fury that the ship could no longer bear up. And the land, the island where passengers and crew might have spent the winter in comparative safety, relentlessly dropped back. The euroclydon, the stormy east-north-east wind of winter, was upon them.

The captain was forced to swing his ship off and with the long oar-like starboard rudder down and the port one triced up he steered a course for the small island of Cauda twenty miles to the south.

The waves striking the rocks and islets off Cauda flung sheets of water, no longer blue, towards the leaden clouds as they rounded the precipitous eastern end. Under the lee of the four-mile stretch of shoreline in calmer water before they drifted away they hauled the ship's boat alongside and, after much difficulty, for it had been swamped, hoisted it on board. Thus they saved the boat which in their haste and optimism they had left in tow.

At the same time the captain, recognizing the stresses which the mounting seas would impose upon his vessel if the storm continued, decided that now was the time, in the only lee he would get, to undergird her if he could. A small hatch in the eyes of the ship was opened and the heaviest mooring ropes hauled from below. These were looped over the bow and, as she rose and forged forward, they were dropped down under her forefoot and allowed to slip along the keel. Three hawsers were placed at intervals around the hull, led through the bulwark rails, brought together on deck and hauled taut by the many hands. They had undergirded their vessel. Her timbers would open less under wracking stresses.

By this time they were losing sight of Cauda in the spindrift to windward as they had lost sight of Crete. Since there was no more land to protect her the captain gave way and let her run before the storm taking the seas with her stern. And there was no direction she could follow but where the wind chose.

After several hours, to relieve the pressure on the mast and to slow the ship down, the captain ordered the mainsail taken in. Paulus watched the almost naked sailors on the great yard, their bare feet gripping the swaying foot-ropes, furling the thick cloth. No more would he see the colourful heraldic arms quartered on the big white sail: the Imperial eagle; Annona, goddess of harvests; the ear of wheat and the eye of the keen-sighted lynx.

More men swarmed aloft as a goat's hair clew line parted under the strain of the thrashing folds. Paulus marvelled at their holding powers while the yard arm dipped towards the water and then swung upwards to the sky. They held what they had captured until the forward pitch of the vessel lightened its weight, then furled another part. They were young and strong and when they had at last secured its full length of almost fifty feet they furled the red topsails.

Below them there were 200 men on the open deck. Some watched those above them on the yard, some looked out over the white-streaked sea, others crouched to avoid the whipping wind. None were comfortable though it was not cold. Seasickness made some disinterested in things around them. Paulus was one who felt ill but the hardships of his life and his will to carry on enabled him to give the appearance of suffering little.

The sailors struck the artemon too, the low bow sail, before it was blown away. As they did so the ship turned slowly, rolled desperately, shipping solid water across the deck. Gradually she assumed a position with the wind and sea on the bow. The high stern in contrast to the low bow held her to the wind in this position, wallowing and at the mercy of whatever came.

To reduce the top-weight the captain had the main yard sent down and secured on deck.

That night the gale continued and in the morning, when the sight of the high, fast-travelling waves with their breaking crests revealed the danger that beset the ship, consternation began to make itself felt in the ranks.

The captain spoke of another peril as Paulus and Julius stood with him on top of the cabin house before the unmanned tillers of the now useless rudders.

"Though they are yet a long way off, the sands of Libya may lie in our path. The direction of the wind when I observed it while running between Crete and Cauda was east-north-east. That would take us into the Gulf of Syrtis and the shallows offshore. But they are several hundred miles away and this heavy vessel is not drifting fast, as you see by the seas that are going by her. If the wind turns to the north-east we shall be on the coast of Cyrenaica much sooner...and that is a rocky coast."

"But the euroclydon comes out of the east sometimes, does it not?" Paulus asked.

"It can do that. If it does it will be better. It might be east now, but I cannot tell."

"This storm cannot last," said the centurion. "I am told it seldom does, even in the midst of winter."

Enveloping spray came over the waist and lashed them. Paulus felt pity for the men on the crowded deck. There was little shelter. The softened skin of the prisoners was obviously being stung by the cutting salt.

By afternoon the ship was pitching violently and rolling too when she had her broad shoulder to the sea. The waves grew longer and higher and every now and then one boarded and swept down the deck among the people. Lifelines were rigged the full length of the deck on both sides to provide additional handholds. The undergirding ropes were frequently tended and when they stretched were tautened with tackles. The two large pumps were manned and water constantly drawn from them.

Before dark the situation became grave. The captain, having watched the ship's behavior, her stability, or lack of it, lying hove to under bare spars in the running sea, no longer under command, decided that she must be lightened. He spoke to Julius of the danger of foundering, a prospect never willingly declared by a master, and sought his agreement to strip the troops of their heavier arms. To this Julius grudgingly acquiesced. The captain then ordered all baggage and military equipage, at the discretion of the centurion, and all heavy stores, even food, to be thrown overboard. The bags of grain could not be discarded. If the hatches were opened the boarding seas would pour down the holds and the water-logged cargo would then swell and spring the sides of the ship. The purpose of under-girding would most certainly be defeated.

Following this the sailors jettisoned the long heavy mainyard with its great square sail, a hazardous and difficult task in the conditions and one which was seen to be the surrender of their chief motive power.

Their plight was as perilous the next day. The sea ran high. Squalls brought driving rain often preceded by thunder and forks of lightning that split the black clouds. Groups of men in turns were allowed to shelter in the great-cabin. They were permitted to occupy the navigation deck above the cabin and the quarter deck which were drier; but not the overhanging gallery for fear it would be carried away by the sea.

More had to be done to bring the ship higher out of the water. The boat the captain would not part with. He concluded he must cut away the mast. And in doing so the constant strain which its swinging motion placed upon the timbers would also be relieved.

Seamen with knives were placed at the lanyards of the shrouds; the stays were loosened. The deck was cleared amidships. Axes bit into the foot of the mast; but its girth was the size of a barrel. With four men on the heaving deck at the axes the moment came. As the ship rolled to port an order rang out. The four starboard shrouds were severed below the deadeyes.

With the sound of splitting above the roar of the storm the great mast fell, the twenty-three-foot topmast with it, crushing the rail where it crashed. As the stays were let go it went by the board before the ship came up from her roll. The port shrouds were cut away and the mast with its tangled rigging was taken by the sea.

Now it was the heavy emblem that adorned the stern, the gracefully curved neck and gilded head of the swan rising fifteen feet above the quarter-deck. Its sudden destruction was like the collapse of a Greek column in an earthquake and left a strange emptiness. Every man on board witnessed this lifesaving massacre of the acrostole with misgivings or outright fear. But the released top-weight had its affect. Greater buoyancy was evident; fewer seas came over the rails.

All that could have been done to save the vessel had been done. The foremast might have been cast overboard as well but it held the only spar to which a sail could be bent in the remote event it could be used. Moreover, the mast's angle, leaning out like a bowsprit, was not the pendulum the massive mainmast had been.

For many days the grain ship lay in the tempest, lifting her laden weight ponderously over the on-rushing waves and pounded by their crests when her slow roll met their approach awkwardly; sliding down the hills of water, floundering and waiting in the spume-streaked troughs to rise again and face the windswept spindrift of another onslaught. The whine of the wind in the rigging that had often risen to a shriek was mercifully gone; there was no rigging. But the creaking of the timbers was all the more audible as the long hull hogged at the wave-tops and torqued when she lay in the valleys of the white-streaked grey seas, half pitching, half rolling. The undergirding helped but it was known that the hull was opening.

The pumps no longer worked; their pipes in the bilges had evidently clogged with wet and matted grain.

Conditions on the crowded deck were distressing and cheerless. Many were weakened and chilled and had given up hope, and the prospects of survival seemed to justify their despair. They had had almost no nourishment; most had lost their desire for food. The fire forward had long since been quenched; the braziers and racks lay cold and wet.

In the makeshift sick bay in the great-cabin, Lucanus had tended those in a poorer state with such liniments and medicines as he still had and with encouragement and tenderness born of his love and compassion for men.

He kept an eye, too, on his manuscript, *The Gospel According to St. Luke*. As long as the ship remained afloat it would stay with him; if the ship sank he would set it adrift. It was in two halves sealed in jars.

There had been some discussion about the safety of the manuscript at the beginning of the voyage when Paulus had spoken of it to the captain and told him of Lucanus's ability as a diarist and historian. A valuable gift Paulus had said and briefly described what Lucanus had recorded. "While we were incarcerated at Caesarea," he explained, "our brother Lucanus, who was free of course, spent much of those two years enquiring into the life of a great man, the greatest of men, Jesus by name. Lucanus travelled through the regions and tramped the roads which He once trod. He spoke to people who had know Him. It was not difficult for them to remember what He had said; He said it so clearly. It was only twenty-five years or so ago. And he wrote it all down on papyrus, in Greek, of course. I know that the narrative has fullness and order, and the research Lucanus did has made it accurate." Paulus had said that he, as much as Lucanus, hoped no harm would befall the manuscript. The captain had asked how it was being carried and Paulus told him the jars were wrapped in straw to prevent damage from ship movement and carried in a net specially made by a fisherman. They had felt fairly confident of its safety.

But now it was less a matter of whether the jars would be smashed as whether the manuscript would survive the sea. Lucanus had recently suspended the net from a beam so that it could swing freely.

The question of where they were was constantly before them. The captain seemed fatigued, more so than the others; more weary than his crew. But he had the burden of responsibility and, though normally agile of body and mind, he was an old man, too old to be thrown and jolted interminably on a lurching deck. The time had passed when they would have struck the sands of Libya, so they had not been blown far south but, rather, to the west. Where, though, was west and where was south? There was no means of knowing. The cloud rack had revealed neither sun nor stars. There was nothing to gauge the wind's direction.

"I have never seen a gale last so long," the captain told Paulus as he looked out over the driven sea with tired eyes. "We must have travelled a long way...But how far?" He lifted his bent shoulders in a questioning shrug. "The deep-sea currents are set by the wind and they will have carried us a hundred miles to leeward apart from the gale's influence. To the westward I suppose."

Paulus could not help him then.

It was dark in the great-cabin. Paulus lay on his back wrapped loosely in his thick brown goat's-hair cloak, his hands clasped on his chest. Thus, with his elbows out and with his legs apart, his body did not turn far as the ship rolled from side to side. Water periodically trickled by him. In spite of bailing and mopping the cabin was always wet. He could sometimes hear, over the complaining cry of the wind outside and the creaking within, and almost feel, the other sleepers lying uneasily near him, their heads towards the bow. He alone seemed wakeful. He watched a long thin triangle of light appear, widen, then disappear as the curtain of the sick bay swung rhythmically. Lucanus wanted the torch for a patient. He watched for its coming with each roll. Paulus thought of Lucanus, his great value as a physician, his gift for careful writing. The long documented narrative he had with him. Would it and all his painstaking research be lost now with the ship? How much longer could they go on? Could the ship hold together? Such a lasting storm! Where...

The shaft of light seemed brighter than it had been. It stayed steady as though the ship had not rolled back to close the curtain. Yet Paulus still moved from side to side on his cloak, the pressure of his body coming on one arm and leg, then on the other. The light, whiter, more silver now, came towards him. It stopped at his feet.

Paulus sat up, his hands behind him flat on the deck. He heard his name spoken.

"Paul..." It was his shortened name, used only by his kin.

"Yes," he whispered..."Yes," he said again in a stronger voice...

In the morning Paulus asked that the whole ship's company be mustered so that he could speak to them briefly. Neither the centurion nor the captain questioned him on what he proposed to say or denied him the authority to say it.

Standing at the break of the cabin house looking at the wet and forlorn gathering swaying below him, his voice rang out in the low Roman tongue above the sounds of wind and sea.

"Friends, if you had listened to me and not put out from Crete, you would have spared yourselves all this damage and loss." He glanced at Julius, the captain and his officers. But there was no animosity in Paulus's eyes, no implication in his speech of foolishness on their part; just pity that they had not heeded his advice. "But now I ask you not to give way to despair. There will be no loss of life at all, only of the ship. Last night there stood beside me an angel of the God to whom I belong and whom I serve, and he said, 'Do not be afraid, Paulus. You are destined to appear before Caesar, and for this reason God grants you the safety of all who are sailing with you.' So take courage, friends; I trust in God that things will turn out as I was told. But we are to be stranded on some island."

Paulus repeated what he had said in Greek.

Men gazed at him in wonderment, at the face that seemed to some no longer ordinary, unprepossessing. To them it shone with beauty, unblemished by the scars. A few, however, appeared unmoved, unwilling to believe the news that others grasped. A mist covered Julius's eyes. Standing with him in the front rank Lucanus and Aristarchus were smiling. Relief and renewed strength seemed to gather in the captain. He was glad to believe the orator.

Behind them the rain-filled clouds thinned and an amber light fell in an ellipse upon the sea. Faintly through the racing rack a watery sun gleamed fleetingly. As Julius turned and dismissed the company he, and those who turned forward, observed a rainbow arched over the eastern sky. Before the others saw it it faded and was gone.

At dusk on the fourteenth day the sea turned from dark grey to murky green and as darkness wore on it became confused. The motion of the ship was short; she tumbled under a new turbulence. It was sensed that the water had shallowed, that land was near.

About midnight the captain called for soundings. The lead was cast and struck bottom at twenty fathoms. After an interval soundings were taken again. The leadsman reported fifteen fathoms.

At the same moment the captain became aware of a new sound, faint and distant, different from the many voices of the storm. The blood pounded in his ears as he struggled to separate the vague rumble from the din he had become so used to. Like a pressure wave it came a little louder, then faded. It was... the boom of surf.

He did not wait. Orders rang out to anchor—to anchor by the stern.

Four small anchors aft were unlashed and cast overboard simultaneously. As their flukes gripped the bottom their rope cables were veered, then held. Gradually the ship's bow swung off to leeward. But as the stern came up into the wind, arrested by the anchors, the weakened overhanging gallery was hit by the upthrust of an enveloping wave and washed away. The sailors belaying the ropes escaped the destruction but, under the flare of the torches, the sight of the wreckage borne by the breakers down the sides of the ship did nothing to strengthen the confidence of those on the fore deck.

Moored in this position the captain was ready to sail down wind and beach her, if beach there was.

Paulus offered up a prayer. The centurion, seeing him thus, waited briefly until he had finished.

"Brother Paulus." It was the first time Paulus had ever heard Julius use such a term of relationship. "Will you pray with the whole ship's company for their preservation until daylight?"

Paulus agreed without hesitation. All hands were assembled.

Standing above them, as he had before, at the break of the cabin deck, seen against the broadly wavering lights only as a short figure wrapped in a heavy Cilician cloak, his arms reaching up, the prisoner of Rome prayed in the voice that had carried so often over great crowds. They heard him and many joined in as best they knew. They saw that this man of the Jewish God, this man of the Christian's Christ, was a man of courage when terror had invaded their own hearts.

But not all were convinced. Paulus, who had remained on the cabin deck after his prayer, was suddenly shocked at what he seemed to see, with his uncertain vision, going on below him. Though his limbs were stiff he leapt down the ladder shouting at several men at the port rail. Then he went quickly into the great-cabin. There he was thankful to find the centurion.

"Julius," he shouted angrily. "Come on deck. They are trying to launch the boat."

Julius burst through the doorway followed by the captain.

They found the boat had already been lowered into the water, an awkward task in the absence of the main yard tackle. But they had done it. Several sailors were in the boat which was tossing violently and crashing dangerously against the ship's side. The men were getting the oars out and were about to cast off.

"Unless these men stay in the ship," Paulus roared over the clamour, "no one can be saved."

"Hold the boat." Julius called to the men.

"What are you doing there?" the captain yelled down.

A voice came up, "Going to lay out the bower anchor."

"You are not. No one gave that order. Come out of it at once. Come up on deck."

The men, seeing they could not escape, climbed up the ropes.

To prevent any further attempt to abandon ship the centurion instructed a soldier to cut the ropes. The only boat they had drifted away.

The gale seemed to moderate before dawn, the ship rode well to her anchors and being stern on was drier. Paulus enquired about food. He suggested they bring up what they could find in the after store. This was done and a modest quantity taken out on deck. But few were concerned with eating, the distant thunder of the surf, more audible now in the dying gale, twisted their already shrunken stomachs and denied them the urge to eat.

Paulus, mounting the ladder to the cabin deck, addressed the men once again, his strong voice drifting over the shambles before him.

"For weeks you have been in suspense; you are tortured and weakened." Day was breaking; they could see him more clearly. "Take something to eat. Now. You need all the strength you can get for the final ordeal facing you. Yet your safety is not in doubt. Not a hair of your heads will be lost. No one will die. Eat what you can."

Etched against a streak of purple above the dark skyline Paulus took some bread, gave thanks to God before them all and broke it. He ate... and so did they.

When he came down on deck again men asked him questions: "Where are we? Is this an island? Who is your god? We knew of Him but do not know Him. Shall we be rescued... saved... save ourselves? You must know how this will happen."

Paulus comforted them. "Trust what I have told you for it has been revealed to me. When we are all safe on shore—and I say all—I shall ask you to recall this moment—you will not forget it—and I shall expect you to be thankful—to my God. And I shall tell you more of Him."

As dawn widened the circle around them and revealed the turmoil of the sea more clearly, all hands, including the soldiers, were ordered to discharge cargo. It mattered no longer if water poured down into the vessel: seepage through the hull had already soaked the grain in the bottom and at the sides. The two hatches were uncovered and those with the strength hauled up bags of wheat, slid them across the deck as it canted down and threw them over the side. There was relief in work. There was a revival of courage through the food they had eaten, damp though it was. There was hope from the words of the squat, almost deformed little man with, to some, the face of an angel.

When they had lightened the ship of as much cargo as could be reached and battened the hatches down again the men turned their attention once more to their perilous position. There, not a mile to leeward, lay the dim outline of land, fading mistily in the rain squalls and returning to view more frighteningly. The scene was such that the chances of survival looked extraordinarily remote.

Presently, in a clear spell, they picked out on the spume-riven shore a smear of tawny beach. And running in on it was what seemed to be the long white wind-whipped surf of a wild sea. It was as though they could see the sickening moan they had heard in the night.

They made it out to be a bay, mainly a rock-strewn bay. Neither the captain nor the officers could recognize it.

"Is this the island you spoke of, Paulus?" the captain asked above the wind.

"Yes."

"Or is it the mainland?"

"It is not." Paulus tightened the girdle of his flapping garment.

"What island is it then?"

"Why do you ask, Captain?" It was Lucanus who spoke, always standing nearby, his stylus and tablet hanging from his belt. "Is it not enough that we have found land before foundering? Paulus said we would reach an island."

"Forgive me, Paulus." The captain appeared old and worn. He looked again at the land. Then as though listening to the sound of the passing sea, the hiss of the combers, the crescendo of their breaking, he seemed to judge the distance... the distance to the point where his ship should ground on the shelving beach—if she missed the rocks. He would be struggling with the torment of driving the passengers, soldiers and prisoners into the surf. At length he spoke.

"I shall beach her. The wind is right. If I wait till it lessens it may change direction and then we may never reach the shore."

The two rudders were lowered from their triced up position; they gripped the water almost down to the keel. Their tillers were manned.

An order was given by an officer standing beside the captain on his platform above the cabin house. In response to it the men in the bows ran the yard of the artimon out along the leaning foremast and the powerful square sail took the wind. The battered hulk strained under its pressure pointing dead to leeward.

Even now, with the slimness of survival facing them, the Augustan Cohorts saw more certain death in a distant land if they allowed their prisoners to escape. They appealed to their centurion to be permitted to kill them. But Julius would not part with Paulus's life. He had a responsibility to Caesar. Moreover, he did not want to incur displeasure in allowing a Roman citizen to be killed. Above all he knew that Paulus would never attempt to escape. And, of course, if he preserved the life of one he must preserve the lives of all the prisoners. He forbade his soldiers to lift a hand against them.

The crew made ready to give up the ship. Axes severed the cables aft. The ship parted from her four anchors. She gathered way quickly and as she went with the wind its sound lulled. She steered unswervingly for the beach in the bay.

All hands were ordered aft in the hope that the keel would take the strand farther up.

The shore came fast towards them as the ship drove in. Lines of foam crinkled the beach, the noise of the surf became louder. She reached the outer breakers, leaned forward and plunged on.

Suddenly she brought up... The whole company were thrown forward. The ship had run aground too soon. A sand bank had lain in her path.

But she did not broach to. She seemed poised to go on, yet her keel held fast, wedged deep in the bank.

Then it was seen that her stern was free. It tried to lift with the rise of the sea, fall with its send, but could only drive shocks through the length of the hull. Half her keel was aground, half still afloat.

Breaking of timbers was heard over the tumult. The quarterdeck was opening, the great-cabin splitting.

The order was passed to abandon ship.

The centurion's voice was heard. All who could swim must strike out on their own; those who could not must seize what they could and drift to the shore. There was flotsam for all as the stern broke up.

When the final count was taken on the beach they numbered 276. Not one had been lost. And as Paulus, almost naked like the others, looked out at the destruction of the derelict, once a liner of the famous Roman grain fleet, he noticed that the sea between the sand bank and the beach was only ruffled, while the surf still rushed in on either side. The bank which held the wreck was as a reef protecting a narrow lagoon inside it.

> "And when they were escaped, then they knew that the island was
> called Melita (Malta). And the barbarous people shewed us no
> little kindness: for they kindled a fire, and received us every one..."

Fire

The ship lifted slowly, gently, listed a little and, with a sigh at her bow where the water parted, lowered herself into the embrace of the ground-swell. She had cleared Durban's long breakwater and was standing out into the Indian Ocean. Captain Arthur Wheeler was almost unaware of the motion as his eyes moved from the men washing down the deck to the pilot boat lolling in the middle distance ahead. The collier was heavily laden, down to her marks again now that she had bunkered.

Captain Wheeler settled his vessel on an east-south-east course and told the second mate to give the engine-room a double ring on the telegraph to signal her final departure from harbour; then he went into the chart-house through the open starboard door. At the high smooth table above the drawers of chart folios he laid off his initial course on a chart that described the coast of southern Africa on one side and Australia on the other. The SS *King Cadwallon* was bound for Adelaide with 7,000 thousand tons of coal. And although she had loaded in midsummer in the Firth of Forth, she was now in midwinter. It was July, 1929. She must not go too far south—must not follow the great circle, but rather strike a rhumb-line across the meridians at the latitude of the Cape of Good Hope.

Wheeler had been master of the *King Cadwallon* for four years and was still only in his middle thirties; and they had been together when he had been mate of her before that. He knew her intimately. Hardly a rivet in her upper deck had escaped his notice at one time or another. He had been thrown out of his big bed as he had been flung out of the mate's bunk when she had been rolling in the quarterly seas coming up from the roaring forties. But the *King Cadwallon* had not always carried coal to Australia. She had tramped all over the world in her nine years of life, sometimes in the grain trade, sometimes with lumber. Wheeler had felt the biting cold off Newfoundland and the Aleutians; he had sweated beneath the awnings on the same teakwood bridge in the tropics.

The *King Cadwallon* had been built in Hong Kong in 1920 and her construction was strong and good. She was well finished too, except, as was usual, in the crew's quarters forward—the fo'c'sle had the customary barren steel nakedness which the heart of the sailor was supposed to enjoy, or at least accept. She was a well-deck steamer of 5,138 tons and had a speed of eight knots, though that was the optimistic speed; her most prominent

King Cadwallon at East London before the fire.

feature was her large black-topped yellow funnel. She was named after an ancient Welsh prince, as were other ships of the firm.

The collier steamed on in her purposeful fashion for six days. Long weed had grown on her sides and bottom, reducing her rate of progress to barely seven knots. Except for two whalers making for Durban with their catches chained alongside, no other vessels were sighted. The weather was moderate, mostly cloudy, and the sea not unkind. She rolled modestly, sometimes loping into a ponderous pitch when the waves came more directly from astern. General good feeling prevailed among the officers and men. Captain Wheeler was easy to get on with. Sitting at the head of the oval table at meals in the saloon he generally kept the conversation among the officers amicable and light. But at dinner on the sixth day of the voyage it was not light.

The mate, at the captain's left side, looked up from his plate. "If it was heavy weather we could take the hatches off and let the sea pour down."

"Even if we could, I wouldn't yet," the captain observed.

"It happens," remarked the chief engineer laconically. He sat on the settee opposite the mate, and having made the brief comment he put down his knife and fork, rose on his short legs and turned, knee on the cushion, and looked out of the forward porthole. After a minute, during which the captain went on eating silently, the chief twisted back and sat down. "Slight yet," he said.

That morning, they had noticed wisps of smoke coming from the after ventilators of No. 2 hold. They had watched from the bridge, a good vantage point. Ragged puffs had appeared creeping out of the cowls. They had turned the forward ventilators' backs to the wind to cut the draught. The two thermometers had been pulled up from the lower hold and the readings compared with those recently recorded in the log book. The starboard one was distinctly high.

Captain Wheeler's blond brows knitted as he drank his tea. Lowering his cup, he said, "We'll just watch it, Chief. May go on like that for a long time. Slight heating somewhere. We had the same situation in No. 2 hold away back when I was mate aboard. Smoked most of the way across here, about three weeks anyway, and I remember the dockers in Adelaide wanted double pay to unload her. Good and hot she was; fire-engines down on the wharf and all."

That afternoon the captain ordered the ventilators to be plugged and covered. By eight bells at the beginning of the first watch the starboard thermometer was higher still, and the other one, on the port side of the hold, which had not previously registered anything significant, was rising. But the night was not an uneasy one for Wheeler. He slept well in the large four-poster in his cabin on the lower bridge, being wakened only when notified of the temperatures at the change of the watches. He was accustomed to danger; it always lurked just over the horizon. On the high seas he went to meet it only when it came directly towards him.

In the morning the canvas cover was taken off one of the ventilators. As the wooden plug was being removed from inside the cowl, black smoke poured out in such volume that it was obvious that the exclusion of air was abortive; spontaneous combustion was in action.

The captain went down and joined the mate on the foredeck. He sent for the chief engineer. Together they watched the carpenter knock the wedges out of one side of the big hatch and the bosun and hands of the watch haul back the three heavy tarpaulins. A hatch-cover was lifted.

They had to stand back as the acrid fumes of smouldering coal met their nostrils. Smoke rose above the derricks and was wafted away on the wind. In turn they looked down the hatch as it cleared away. They would have to take off the 'tween-deck hatches to see anything more.

"How about steam, Chief?" Wheeler asked, stepping back to the bulwark. His tall slim figure contrasted with the chief's as the engineer moved away from the hatch and looked up at him.

"Steam?"

"Yes. Steam might have a good effect."

"It might smother it. But it may be seated pretty deep."

"Maybe. Hard to tell. Could you get steam down?"

After a pause, the chief, looking along the deck and at the hatch, agreed that he could.

They gained access to the lower hold, laid a steam line down and covered up. One unfavourable aspect was that No.2 was the largest hold in the ship and much penetration was needed.

As the day wore on, apprehension grew with the rising temperature of the hold. But perhaps the steam had something to do with that. In the middle of the afternoon they shut off the steam and opened up the hatch again to see the effectiveness of the hot damp cloud. As they did so, thick smoke billowed out, just as though it were coming from the funnel when the ship was steaming hard. They shut down in haste and turned on the steam once more.

Captain Wheeler went into the chart-house. It was the place to which he gravitated unconsciously when he wanted to think, to weigh matters, to make decisions. He stood staring at the chart, not seeing what was before him. He had never known a fire take hold of a cargo of coal so quickly. He had experienced small bunker fires and heated cargoes before—had he not travelled half-way to Australia along this same course with smouldering coal in that very hold and held it in check for weeks? But who or what had really held it in check?

Had he not ventilated the hold enough? They had come a long way from the doldrums where air movement was slight. Had he ever read of combustion in coal gaining strength as quickly as this—in a matter of a day or two? It seemed that he had—somewhere. He began to think that he ought to inform his owners of the situation. But was it really grave? Was he unduly anxious? If nothing serious came of it and the steam held the fire down, or put the smouldering menace out, he would appear foolish, an alarmist.

He took off his gold-peaked cap and dropped it on the chart, pushing his long fingers through his fair hair. Should he go on or turn back?

To turn back when he had steamed almost a thousand miles would be an economic dead loss. On the other hand he had 4,000 miles to go, or in an emergency 3,000 to the nearest port in Australia, Fremantle. Then again, communications would become more difficult as the distance from Africa increased. In fact, they would vanish; radio range was short, often erratic. They would meet no ships after this—none travelled to Africa in these latitudes against the wind. Moreover, if gales blew, and they were normal at this time of the year, it would be harder to get back. Such moderate weather as this seldom prevailed.

He would give it another two hours.

As dusk fell he was back in the chart-house. It was fire at sea! There was no doubt of its virulence now. Obnoxious gas fumes were seeping through the plugged ventilators.

"Nine hundred and fifty miles," Wheeler repeated as the second mate measured off the distance along the course line. The second mate, officially the navigator, drew a small circle round the dot on the chart, spread his dividers to the nearest parallel and meridian, and made a note of the latitude and longitude.

"Position's pretty accurate, I think, Sir," he said. "Sights this morning were fair."

In the silence that followed, the captain's only movement as he stood erect at the open lee door, his clenched fists deep in his reefer pockets, was the rhythmic sway of his body to the roll of the heavy vessel. He saw the desolate track ahead leading deeper into the heart of the Southern Indian Ocean: he saw the wind-swept miles astern offering resistance to a ship plugging into the westerlies. To him it may have been as though he were watching a child in a fever, his own child, exposed to wind and rain, unable to take shelter, shivering outside, burning inside.

"Should advise the owners," the second mate heard him say indistinctly. But his mind could not really have been on them. The ship was his; he and she had been together always. Everywhere she went, everything she did, was for him. Her destiny was his to protect. Although in the company of other men, he and she were spiritually alone—in mutual companionship.

Suddenly he withdrew his hands from his pockets, stepped over the high sill of the door and strode to the teakwood rail of the bridge. He glanced ahead, then back beyond the wake where, in the fading light, an albatross was gliding massively.

"Port," he said in a steady tone to the third mate.

The officer passed the order to the man at the wheel and the *King Cadwallon* began to turn.

"Come right round." He gave the compass course to steer.

He sent word to the mate that the ship was turning and to the chief engineer to give her all the steam he could raise. He pulled up the canvas dodger in front of him as the wind caught the fore part of the bridge and cooled his face. When she was settled on her new course he went into the chart-house again and wrote on a piece of paper, 'On fire No. 2 hold. Returning Durban.' The owners must know. So must Lloyd's of London.

Night fell. They hesitated to lift the hatches for inspection again, because of the greater draught the bow wind would induce below decks. But in the middle watch, with the temperature still rising, they tried to go down. Steam and smoke drove them back.

At first light they abandoned steam and turned to that great fire repellent, water—not fresh water; that was needed for the boilers. The hoses, already coupled up in readiness, were aimed down the hold and the pump in the engine-room worked to capacity. That seemed better and hopes rose, but fresh air was being admitted too. Men took it in turns to tend the hoses at the weather hatch-coaming while the smoke coiled out of the lee side. The coal pile below looked like the sulphurous outcrop of a volcano.

All that day, during the night and the day that followed, the flow of water through the nozzles was kept going constantly. As a stream of water was shifted to another part of the heaped mass, threads of smoke wove up through the wet shining nuggets where the hose had been playing before. It was impossible to tell where the seat of the fire was, or its true extent, or even whether they were successfully holding it down. As draughts caught the surface of the pile the smoke would flatten down, then surge up again. Sometimes, as the ship pitched, the belching became heavier and gave the impression that it was being generated from the bottom.

In the late afternoon of the second day of back-tracking some of the crew said they thought they had heard sounds below. The chief engineer, who had spent all his seagoing life burning coal, believed the fire had such a thorough hold that the puny streams of water could not quench it.

"It's deep down somewhere," he said, as he and the captain and the mate stood by the opening looking down.

"Probably," Wheeler agreed. "By the heat of No. 1, I think it's in the fore end. But even if we knew for certain, there's nothing more we can do."

He had searched very carefully through his experience of nearly twenty years to see if there was anything he might do that he had left undone. There was nothing.

"Sometimes when I watch it," said the mate, "I don't know whether it's getting better or worse. It's like looking into fog; you often think it's clearing a bit when it's not."

Before full light the next morning, the fourth morning since smoke first appeared, the mate on the bridge heard a cry from one of the men at the hoses; he thought he had shouted "Flames." He hastened down the ladders and dropped onto the fore well-deck. In the dimness he saw two or three tongues of flame flickering under the fore part of the hatch on the starboard side.

"Just saw it dancing around there as I swept along with the hose," one of the seamen said. "Couldn't have been burning long or I'd have see'd it afore."

"It's got us now!" breathed the mate. "Keep your hoses around there." The men did not need to be told.

He went up to the captain's cabin.

That was when Wheeler sent the SOS. With it he asked for immediate assistance and gave his position as latitude 32° 01' south, longitude 40° 41' east.

The wireless operator got the message off at once, then repeated it. The air had been silent, but as they drew nearer the coast, traffic should be heard. Operators would be coming on watch at eight o'clock on single-operated ships. He sent the message twice more.

Then he heard a clear answer. Morse conversation followed for a minute. The captain, on his way up from the foredeck, had stepped into the wireless office and was listening to the tapping key. When it stopped the operator swung round.

"*Ardenhall* answers, Sir."

"How far away do you think she is?"

"Not too far. Signals are strong. Within 200 miles I should think. The operator's gone to get their position."

The answering steamer's position, when they plotted it on the chart, revealed her to be 150 miles to the north. The *Ardenhall* said she was turning to the southward; and she asked for the *King Cadwallon's* course and speed so that she could intercept. The details were flashed across the sea and it was arranged that wireless direction-finding would be used when they came within range.

By mid-morning the whole of No. 2 hold was aflame and its heat had ignited No. 1. The fire had caught very quickly in the foremost hold, evidently transmitted by the watertight bulkhead in red heat.

With the appearance of flames in No. 2 the smoke lessened but the heat increased. No. 1 smoked heavily. They coupled two more hoses to the water line which ran just above the port scuppers, to try to contain No. 1; but this reduced the pressure on all four hoses. Nevertheless four streams of water were used. The fire in No. 2 hold did not leap out of the hatch; it seemed to burn steadily with a low flickering. To Wheeler the sight was alarming. Could they keep it from gaining strength until they reached port? He remarked to the mate as he watched the dancing flames that it hardly seemed likely. "And there's 2,500 tons of coal under that fire." As it was, sufficient heat was being thrown up the hatch to cause the men to stand well back. The upper deck was growing very hot.

For the first time the captain had to admit the possibility of abandoning ship—the saddest phrase a master can use. Yet he had to advise his owners in his report that morning that it might happen.

The early morning SOS had been intercepted by Jacobs's wireless station at Durban, and this had at once prompted the Admiral commanding the station to dispatch his flagship, HMS *Calcutta*, to the rescue. Wheeler, however, informed the cruiser that he would have the help of the *Ardenhall* long before the Navy could reach him. This created a stir in the Natal city and people waited for further word from the ship in distress.

Captain Wheeler altered course to north-west to bring the hour of rendezvous nearer. He could not steer more to the north because that would bring the wind ahead, and if the flames rose they would sweep the bridge.

By ten in the morning the two ships had bearings of each other, and soon after the second mate came up to the bridge from dinner he sighted smoke on the horizon. As the masts and funnel of the *Ardenhall* came into view minds seemed easier among the crew. But though relieved to know his men were now fairly safe Captain Wheeler expressed a feeling of regret for having diverted a ship on the high seas for protection against what was still just a possibility.

"We might make Durban yet," he said to the mate, and he ordered a flag hoist to be sent aloft asking the rescue vessel to steam along in company.

The mate was beside him. "Afraid it's getting worse, Sir. No. 1 is afire now. You can see it burning."

Wheeler continued to examine the approaching ship. Then he lowered his binoculars and glanced at the mate. "Yes. But we may confine it." He paused as he gazed down on the foredeck. "I don't want to leave her," he said, simply. "I don't want to lose her."

The mate looked away.

The *Ardenhall* was steaming on a parallel course about a mile to windward, but no one aboard the *King Cadwallon* relaxed his efforts. The men seemed more purposeful; the donkeyman tended the pump as assiduously as ever; the steward left the saloon to relieve a seaman at one of the hatches as soon as the last officer had risen from the table; the third engineer went down to the stokehold to encourage the firemen at the furnaces.

Late in the afternoon the flames in No. 2 were licking the hatch-coaming; the coal in No. 1 was glowing, with a rising fire in the after end, while smoke was curling up from the centre of the great pile. The men were ordered to take their belongings out of the fo'c'sle and stow them under the poop. The two lifeboats on the lee side were swung out.

As darkness descended the ship ploughed on, her foremast and rigging lit by the dancing light below, and shadows leaping at the superstructure. Men with blackened faces were coming to the chief steward for petroleum jelly to ease their scorched skin. Wheeler himself had to send for some. The African coast was still nearly 500 miles away.

Soon after four bells the captain sent for the chief engineer. He himself waited in the chart-house with the mate. "We'll go, Chief," he announced. "Shut down, but leave the pump going. We'll take the port boats. They're ready. The crew can take some gear; not much. Muster within half an hour." His words were quietly spoken and without emotion, but his eyes showed what his voice hid.

The furnaces were banked and the ship was stopped: the propeller made its last turn. The captain went to his cabin and knelt at the safe, withdrawing the ship's papers and such money as he was carrying. He pushed them into a bag with the log book and stood up. He dislodged a photograph from a slot built on his desk, dropped it into the bag and snapped it shut.

As he stepped out onto the lower bridge he saw that his boat was ready, with men sitting on the thwarts. The ship was lying beam on to the wind. The light of the fire, now blowing high over the lee bulwark, lit the lifeboat so that the faces of the black firemen could be distinguished from those of the white sailors. There was a dull roar from the holds as the air sucked up the flames. The fire was out of control. Both holds were burning fiercely; flames seared the paint on the derricks and snatched at the crow's-nest.

"Have you counted the hands?" Wheeler asked the second mate.

"Yes, Sir. and the mate's boat's counted. We've thirty-six between us."

"Take my bag and jump in then."

"Lower away," he yelled to the after boat. As he gave the order and repeated it to his own boat a deafening jet of steam burst from the pipe high up on the funnel. The boilers were blowing off. The *King Cadwallon* was having the last word.

In the turmoil of the moving sea the lifeboats were warped aft and the captain and mate, with the hands who had manned the falls, swung down into them as they wallowed against the side. The final act was over. The hurricane-lamps in the sternsheets seemed to dip between the waves and sway over the crests as the oarsmen pulled towards their liberator now lying to leeward; but the flickering lamps were infinitely feeble against the blaze behind.

The *King Cadwallon* was abandoned at eleven o'clock on the night of Thursday, July 12.

On August 5 the steamer *Ripley Castle* came into Port Louis, Mauritius. Her master said he had passed what he thought was the *King Cadwallon* on the night of July 30. He gave her position then as latitude 27° 22' south, longitude 38° 38' east. She was on fire fore and aft. The fire had even got at the bunkers—there were flames rising from the saddleback. He noted that the masts, funnel, derrickposts and upper-structure were still standing; the upper deck hatchbeams were still in position.

The abandoned, fire-ridden derelict must have presented a desolate sight lying on the ocean, her blackened spars swinging slowly across the sky as she rolled—once the home of men.

She had already drifted 260 miles in eighteen days. A south-south-east wind must have taken hold of her. It was one of the flukes of nature that she had not been caught by the prevailing wind and, with the current, swept across the Indian Ocean to the coast of Australia and ultimately back in the Equatorial Current to the north of Madagascar.

Two weeks went by after the sighting made by the *Ripley Castle*. Then the whaler *Egeland* came into Durban. Her skipper said he had boarded the *King Cadwallon* forty miles north-east of the port and found her burnt out, but the fire still smouldering. He had taken her in tow, but had had to let her go when a gale came up.

The next day, August 15, dawned fair, and the *Egeland* cast off again and steamed out to sea. She was attracted by salvage, not whaling. But the minesweeper *Sonnebloom* also went out, under orders to report the condition of the derelict so that a tug might be dispatched. To the mortification of the whaler she could not find the *King Cadwallon*: nor could the *Sonnebloom*.

Two days later she was reported off Bashee with two other whalers hovering in the offing apparently waiting for a chance to take her in tow. Caught in the Agulhas Current, one of the fastest of ocean streams, the *King Cadwallon* had been swept past Durban and in towards the coast two hundred miles to the south at the rate of sixty miles a day.

Finally, on August 19, she was sighted fifteen miles off East London. A government tug was sent out and towed her in, anchoring her in the roadstead at 4:30 the next morning.

From the spot where she was abandoned, well south of Madagascar, the burning ship had drifted north-north-west towards Mozambique, and had then turned south-west to be carried down almost to the foot of Africa before she was caught—a thousand miles from her starting-point—after a journey lasting thirty-eight days.

Now the Salvage Association had a chance to examine the hulk on behalf of Lloyd's. Climbing aboard over the scarred bulwarks from the tender, the surveyor and his assistant dropped down onto a rusted deck devoid of the customary grey paint. Looking along the after well-deck they saw two gaping holes, the two after hatches, their wooden covers and tarpaulins gone. Thin trails of smoke came up from below, but they could see down to the vast pile of ash. Lying grotesquely, half submerged in sulphurous dust, were the great beams, the movable strongbacks which gave transverse strength to the decks, black and twisted. The hatch-coamings were bent inward. Everything on deck was scorched and blackened; no ropes were to be seen; parts of the rigging had melted. Under the poop the steering-gear was shattered.

They mounted a distorted ladder to the midship deck and looked through the open steel engine-room door. Water lapped at the cylinder heads; the space above echoed to their voices. Cabins on deck were open to the elements, only the hinges on the doors left. Inside the accomodation there was ash but no woodwork. The thick glass of the portholes had melted and run down the sides of the cabins.

The surveyor managed to climb down into No. 2 'tween deck. It was warm, and a fire still smouldered. He saw that the side of the ship was buckled below the sheer strake. He came up. The fo'c'sle was gutted; not an awning spar stood above it. There was no bridge, except for a spectre of blackened irregular steel. There was no wheel. The unused weather lifeboats were gone. Nothing but steel could have lived through the fire, and even that had suffered.

Seven thousand tons of coal had been consumed, leaving five smouldering ash-pits.

Lloyd's, whose property she now was, asked the port authorities to bring the derelict right into the East London river for a closer survey. The authorities hesitated; the *King Cadwallon* was still burning and the inner harbour was crowded with ships.

On September 12, she was tugging at her rusty anchor cable, still in the open roadstead, the authorities still refusing to have her within the breakwater. A gale was blowing. In the afternoon she drove ashore. There on the rocks she broke her back, and her fore part, from bridge to bow, sank. Two weeks later, heavy seas ran again and demolished the after part of her hull. On October 8, 1929, three months after she caught fire, the seas pounded her to pieces. All that was left of the wreck above water was the battered ironwork of her stern and her mainmast.

In the course of his wanderings round the world in command of other ships of the fleet, Captain Arthur Wheeler no doubt saw the tangled mound of rusted steel resting against the rocks of East London Roads—a monument to his tragedy. He would have known the ship to which it belonged, though he could not have recognized anything that was once his, or hers. But he would quietly have saluted her remains.

Beyond the Limit

"Ive come for the *Hazel E. Herman,*" Captain Gabriel Pentz said simply as he handed a letter to the tall, well-dressed man seated at a large carved desk.

"The *Hazel Herman?*"

"Schooner."

"Oh, yes. Yes. Let's see. She's lying down there in the dock. Been there for more than a year, I should think." The British consul resident in Mobile, Alabama, tilted back and opened the envelope.

A hot zephyr moved the blind at the open window but did not stir the stagnant air of the handsome office. Mr. Ross let the letter drop on his desk.

"Captain Pentz. You're from Nova Scotia. A lot of captains come from there."

The consul picked up the single sheet of paper again. "She's owned by a Mrs. Amy Rafuse. Is that right?"

"So I was given to understand by her agent before I left home. I was told I'd find Bowman Rafuse here who would act for his wife while the schooner was in Mobile."

"Never heard of the man." The consul spoke sharply which gave Captain Pentz the feeling that the Englishman knew everyone.

Pentz pulled his pipe out of his pocket, thought better of it and shoved it back. "Bowman Rafuse," he muttered. "I was told Bowman would be here." Mr. Ross was gazing out of the window. He swung round.

"Yeoman, perhaps you mean! There is a fellow called Yeoman who has been around Mobile off and on for some time. A Canadian—thus a British subject, of course." He hesitated. "I think, Captain, you had better meet him. I'll see him shortly, no doubt. In the meantime, you might want to look over the *Hazel Herman.* She's going to be released by the customs soon. If I am right about Yeoman it will probably be arranged that you come to me for funds to put the boat in order and for a crew when you're ready to sail."

Captain Pentz left the consul's office with a puzzled frown pulling together the black brows over his bright, experienced eyes and made his way to the docks. The vagueness annoyed him after traveling for days in a train in high summer to the Gulf of Mexico.

Through directions given him he came to what seemed a secluded and little-used wharf, deserted except for the two-masted schooner dozing against the shell-encrusted wooden piles. He recognized her at once. He knew the *Hazel Herman*. She had been built at Snyder's yard at Dayspring just upstream from his home on the LaHave River. He had seen her bringing fish in from the Banks for something like five or six years. Then she had disappeared like so many other schooners in the fishing slump of the 1920s and gone south, they said.

Gabriel Pentz gazed at the schooner with professional appreciation. She was a big vessel, perhaps 130 feet long from her gracefully curved bow to the taffrail at her long undercut stern.

He crossed the narrow plank and dropped to the hard wooden deck. Though broad-shouldered, he was slim and agile for a man of forty-one. It was silent aboard; she was lifeless. Her canvas, still on her booms, was weakened by weather and sun. But her spars were good, her rails solid, her hull would probably be the same. He was not displeased and would be glad to command her if Bowman Rafuse, or Yeoman, if that was his name here, was prepared to put out some money to refit her.

A remark the British consul had made suddenly came to his mind as he strode back through the streets of Mobile to his modest hotel: "She is going to be released by the customs soon." She must have been in trouble! What sort of trouble? Rum running? Pentz had heard from those returning to Lunenburg that rum running had expanded in the Gulf and off the Florida coast in the last two years from a lively illicit trade to an enterprise approaching the magnitude of the gang-controlled violence that had persisted for years in the waters between the Virginia Capes and New England. Had the *Hazel E. Herman* been involved in this?

Well, she was not in it now, and his commission was to sail the vessel home to the LaHave River direct. He had accepted the job for $125 a month and had been paid a month in advance.

The schooner was liberated in less than a week—apparently the courts had 'rationalized' their earlier judgement and found no case against her. During this time Captain Pentz made daily visits to the consul's office in the hope of meeting Bowman Rafuse. He knew what he looked like because he had known him slightly at home; he lived only a few miles from him up the river.

At last Bowman appeared and was introduced by the consul as Mr. Yeoman. There was no mistake, he was the same man, though his name differed in the two worlds.

He had the handsome, carefree appearance he had always had, smiling and affable, and greeted the captain with obvious joy. "I'm glad you got down here. I knew you'd come. No good skippers in the South. I know your reputation—the best."

A small man stood beside him. "This is R.J. Silver. He'll be your supercargo." Pentz shook a weak hand. "You can haul the *Hazel Herman* out into Faber's slipway tomorrow," Bowman went on cheerfully, "and have her bottom scraped and the vessel overhauled. There's plenty of money for

The *Hazel Herman.* . . "was a big vessel, perhaps 130 feet long from her gracefully curved bow to the taffrail at her long undercut stern."

it." He glanced at Mr. Ross who seemed to agree. "Pick up a mate on the waterfront to help you put her on the slip, and you can order a tug. Have all bills sent to Mr. Ross; we'll look after them."

Two weeks later the *Hazel Herman,* in good condition, was at her loading berth. She was taking liquor aboard; Silver was tallying it. Rafuse came down the dock. Captain Pentz was annoyed and worried. He tackled Rafuse.

"I come here to take the vessel back to Nova Scotia light, Bowman, empty, as I understood it. And now you're loading her with rum. Nobody takes that stuff to Nova Scotia."

Bowman Rafuse smiled blithely, "Why, Gabe, I've got to shift it. It was the cargo they seized. It's been released, like the vessel, and I'm obliged to do something with it."

"You own the cargo, too?"

"Er...no,"

Pentz noticed he did not deny owning the schooner. Standing on the wharf together they watched the slings of whisky and rum being hoisted inboard and lowered alternately down the two hatches into the big hold.

"Look, Bowman. I'm ignorant of the rum trade. I've never been in the business as you know."

"That's why I wanted you, Gabe."

"Huh! I don't like it and don't want it."

"There's nothing to it. The supercargo will look after the liquor, he'll be responsible for it. Silver's a good man. He'll do all the paper work as well. You just have to sail the vessel and keep the cargo dry."

"Keep bottles dry!" Pentz nearly cracked the stem of his pipe with his teeth. "And where do I clear for?"

"Tell you what, Gabe. I'll jack up your pay to two hundred dollars a month. How's that? Get the consul to give you a note."

"Is he in it too? I don't want no funny money...nor your bloody rum."

"We'll fix it up at the consul's office in the morning," Rafuse answered as he turned to walk up the wharf.

Gabriel Pentz still wanted to know where he was going but Bowman Rafuse seemed to be in a hurry. Perhaps he had not heard the question; Pentz knew he was genuinely hard of hearing.

The *Hazel Herman* sailed early on July 3. The captain's orders were brief. They were simply to transfer his cargo to a three-masted schooner off Jacksonville, Florida and then proceed to Nova Scotia. Well, at least he would get rid of it fairly soon.

A brassy sun was already heating the fetid atmosphere of the docks when a large customs launch came under the bow and called for a line—the law demanded that a liquor-laden sailing vessel had to be towed out by the customs. The launch towed the schooner four miles down Mobile Bay and then cast off.

Captain Pentz, who was about to order the foresail hoisted, was surprised to see the launch, instead of sheering off, drop back alongside. He was more astonished when two blacks jumped aboard and commenced removing cases of alcohol from his deck and passing them down to the customs officer and a boy in the boat. Silver was standing there and might even have been tallying them as they disappeared.

Pentz felt a tingling at the back of his neck and had difficulty preventing himself from roaring at Silver and particularly at the launch. But he reminded himself that the freight was the supercargo's business. He wished he could have had this liquor-making ingredient stowed below with the rum but alcohol, he had been informed, had to be carried on deck. He wondered if this was a port rule prompted by the customs who were now stealing upwards of 300 cases in front of his eyes. It was a relief to him when the sickening sight of brazen theft broke off, governed only by the capacity of the boat; and the agent of a respected department of the United States government sped away without a word having been spoken or a glance cast at the master of the plundered schooner.

Pentz wasted no time. The donkey winch sputtered, then chugged evenly as the foresail went up, the jib and jumbo were trimmed and the *Hazel Herman* began a slow beat into the light south-east trade wind to clear the bay. The captain watched closely while the heavy mainsail was hoisted, his anger ebbing as his interest grew in his attempt to assess the seamanlike qualities of his crew. The mate and the three deckhands were blacks from Grand Cayman Island. They should be good and they seemed to be. The cook, who joined the seamen when making sail, was not so handy. He was a native of Georgia of French Acadian descent. To the captain's eye he was a mulatto.

It seemed no trouble for the hands to set the mainsail, and the vessel's ability to sail pleased the captain. In the light breeze her canvas pulled her black hull smoothly through the rippling water, her clean lines and sharp stem responding effortlessly to the unshivering set of the sails. Her lee rail was well clear of the water's edge even though she was loaded with what Pentz estimated to be about 3,000 cases of whisky and rum.

Working the schooner to windward with these men brought no confusion, no doubts. They knew the ropes and tackles, were obviously familiar with the rig.

The sailing conditions lifted his spirits from the lower levels of despondency and the morning after departure brought a stiffening breeze with shafts of sunlight piercing the bluer water of the deeper regions of the Gulf.

The *Hazel Herman* passed through the Florida Straits and entered the Atlantic edging north gradually so that her course would take her well off the Florida coast and about equidistant from the Western Bahamas. The proximity of the islands was evident by the fast craft which occasionally crossed her track, their wakes boiling in response to their high-powered motors. Bimini, where rum was plentiful, was a mere dog watch or so from Miami.

Sailing by the wind the vessel heeled gracefully to the light trades. And the captain knew that she was doubling her apparent speed by the lift she had from the invisible north-running Gulf Stream. Such favourable conditions with not much to do gave him time to review the prospects before him. He did so in the light of his stay in the flourishing port of Mobile under Alabama's lightly-accepted enforcement of the unpopular prohibition law of the United States.

He did not like his immediate orders. The schooner with which he was to rendezvous was the *Donald* and the position, twenty-nine miles off St. Johns River bar, below Jacksonville, and thirty-one miles from St. Augustine Inlet. It was well outside the twelve-mile limit though. If the sea were flat he could unload fairly quickly but if it were rough it would take time and subject his vessel to damage; and the other one too, which had its significance.

The orders sounded straight enough but he could not see the object of the transfer. Why shift the rum from one schooner to another? Moreover, he had heard an undercurrent of speculation on the waterfront, now that the *Hazel Herman* was to unfurl her sails. It seemed that no master would take her, and most thereabouts, if not all, were hard-boiled in the rum trade. Was this because of an unsavory past? Or was it her owner's reputation of uncertainty; Yeoman?

Gabriel Pentz had kicked himself several times for having taken the job. But he was in the operation and could not get out of it. He could not have renounced his commission when he discovered the nature of the freight and taken the long journey home because he hadn't the money to return. He had been out of employment for six months and, like most of Nova Scotia's seafarers, had badly needed a job. It had been a period when it was said that hardworking fishermen could loaf with a clear conscience. Pentz had been captain of a tug in the Arctic, then master of coastal steamers for eight years until his firm, the LaHave Steamship Company, was defeated by lack of business. He had four children between the ages of one and ten and while he owned a good house overlooking the river he, like others, could not be idle forever. No, he could not have gone back.

While Pentz speculated his crew were quiet and seemed happy. He wondered why, if the vessel was to return to Canada he had not been instructed to bring a Lunenburg crew with him. It would be much less difficult than coming in to a Nova Scotian port with a foreign crew and trying to repatriate them with the complications that would arise.

The one nuisance was the supercargo. Perhaps Silver had too little to do. He had been reasonably cordial at first through his tough exterior but he had grown morose and snivelling and, of all stupid things, wanted to be put ashore. The shore was a place to be avoided.

Conjecture about the future was of so little use in the captain's untutored knowledge of rum running that he decided he must more or less put it out of his mind until he reached his destination. This was made easier by his sense of felicity when the breeze freshened and his vessel sped like a flying cloud through the sun-flecked sea. No schooner's sails could have drawn better, no hull could have responded to the pressure of the wind with more willingness. Perhaps reliance of her swiftness had once been her downfall.

The *Hazel Herman* reached her rendezvous on the morning of July 15, twelve days out of Mobile Bay. Captain Pentz's spirits were heightened when he saw a schooner lying to under light sail. She was in the approximate position he intended to take up. But then he remembered the vessel he was to meet was a three-master and this was a two-masted schooner like his own. Coming closer he saw she was the *Clark Corkum*. He sailed slowly on ranging the area in a wide circle and scouring the horizon for his consort. She was not to be seen.

The next day he went aboard the *Clark Corkum* to check his sextant against her captain's. He asked the agreeable but occupationally uncommunicative captain if he had seen the *Donald*. "No," he answered. "She's still in Havana, I guess."

For four days Pentz hung around on his position off St. Augustine, sometimes at anchor, sometimes cruising a little farther out or up and down the coast for short distances though not close in. But he did not encounter the *Donald*. Perhaps she really was in Havana.

On the 19th a fast motor boat came out from shore and drew alongside. A man boarded and introduced himself as Jim Clark and said he was to take the rest of the deck cargo of alcohol. "Me and Steve'll fix up the papers," he told the captain.

"Steve? Who's Steve?" Pentz asked.

"Steve Metcalf of course; your supercargo."

"Oh. I thought he answered to the name of Silver."

"Yeah...Yeah." There was some derision in his visitor's voice.

"Umph," growled Pentz. "Silver Steve don't seem to know who he is." But Clark was moving away from the poop to join the supercargo.

As Pentz was glaring at the two men he saw Jim Clark hand a small package to Silver who slipped it into his pants pocket. He determined to keep a close eye on Silver, or whatever he called himself. He was sick of the man's moroseness and complaining.

The boat pushed off when it was well loaded for its 30 mile trip to shore, perhaps more, depending on the backwater it was heading for.

Strangely, Silver's disposition changed. He became serene and pleasant, almost cheerful; his nonsense stopped as though his soul had been cleansed at a gospel meeting.

Soon after noon the following day a schooner hove in sight coming out of Jacksonville and stood towards the *Hazel Herman*. When she was within hailing distance Pentz recognized Bowman Rafuse standing on the poop. He came aboard.

By nightfall they had transferred 800 cases of whisky to the schooner's deck. She then let go and was soon lost in the darkness.

Rafuse remained aboard the *Hazel Herman*. He said he would stay until the *Donald* came to take the rest of the cargo.

A sultry week passed. Rafuse was genial and Pentz found him quite companionable, particularly since the captain had little affinity with anyone else, except in a nautical sense. But his chatter was light and trivial and he never committed himself to any discussion on matters of business or spoke of his personal interests. He drank liberally from a case of rum he had brought up from the hold and seemed to regret that the captain did not join him.

Yet his disappointment appeared to be tempered with some satisfaction that the master of his vessel was a man of temperance.

He annoyed Pentz sometimes with his ignorance of ships, except the capacity of their holds and a rough idea of how long it took to sail from a Caribbean port to the Florida coast. And even this seemed to Pentz somewhat erroneous when it came to speculation about the arrival of the *Donald*.

One afternoon Jim Clark came out again in a fast boat and he and Bowman Rafuse conferred at some length, out of earshot of the captain. When he left he took Steve Metcalf, or Silver, with him.

"Is that the last we're going to see of him?" Pentz asked hopefully.

"Yes," Rafuse answered. "He's joining the *Clark Corkum* as supercargo. We don't need him here. I'll look after the rum."

"Strange guy. Gets as melancholy as hell at times. Seems half crazy."

Rafuse watched the boat retreating. "Hophead," he commented casually.

"Hophead?"

"Hophead."

"Drinks beer?"

"No. Takes drugs. Lots of hopheads around these parts. Dismal characters. Even dangerous when they haven't got their pills."

"Well," said Pentz slowly, "that explains a thing or two." He looked in the direction of the familiar schooner a mile or two away. "Sorry for the *Corkum*. Good fellow, the captain."

But then he noticed another motor boat meet the one Jim Clark and the hophead were in and instead of making over to the *Clark Corkum* they steered in together towards the land.

There were many things Gabriel Pentz could not figure out.

On the 28th a storm came up the coast. When Pentz saw his barometer falling and the state of the sky he steered east on the strengthening breeze. But Rafuse objected to being taken off position.

"I want to be well off the land when the wind comes, as it will," Pentz explained. "Hurricane I reckon."

After a while Rafuse suggested taking shelter in Jacksonville.

"Wouldn't want them harbours in a hurricane," Pentz retorted. "Safer to ride it out at sea. Don't want no palm trees flying around fouling the rigging."

Rafuse pondered. "If we did go in we'd never get out again, of course. Be stuck for another year. No, that would be a mistake."

The hurricane came with its inevitable force and threw the vessel back towards the land. There was no clawing off. The foresail was blown out of its boltropes in the night and the storm sail could not stay her leeway. In the shallows off Halifax Beach Captain Pentz anchored just short of the surf. Though almost never a saving device in a storm he had no alternative. By the grace of God the massive fisherman's anchor, a relic of the Banks, held the schooner.

And so they stayed in the driving winds of a tropical cyclone, thrashing violently in the short precipitous ground sea.

In that period of riding it out Pentz saw another side of Bowman Rafuse. He confined himself to the dim, tumbling cabin and when Pentz had a chance to leave the deck and go below at first light on the second day he was shocked at the decline of the man he had known as debonair, buoyant, carefree.

When Pentz spoke to him he seemed not to hear. His mouth hung open as though his mind was absorbed in the sound of the creaking timbers rasping the humid air of the confined space. There was justification for concern but not such as would drive a man to abject terror. All he got when he tried to encourage Rafuse was the barely audible utterance, "She's foundering-...breaking up," while he stared at the heaving deck as though he was looking through the planks into a maelstrom.

At first Pentz was impatient with him but the plaintive voice struck a chord in the captain that he could not have known was alive in him away from home. To see a shipmate—though a non-professional—collapse with fear left him with some sense of compassion, and because he was the only man of his own kind on board gave him a depressing feeling of loneliness.

But Rafuse did not take to the bottle. Pentz was glad of that, though the thought occurred to him that it might have been better if he had.

The violent pitching eased as the day wore on and the shriek in the rigging turned to an undulating moan. The glum Rafuse recovered quickly as the survival of the vessel became obvious. In the evening the wind came lightly off the land; the hurricane had traveled on. With difficulty the captain broke his anchor out of the clay bottom and by morning had made his offing.

It was August 1, when they took up their position again, this time fifty miles due east of Jacksonville. Between that date and August 9 they jogged off and on, sometimes closing the coast within range of the light at St. Augustine, sometimes standing out beyond the twenty-fathom line, always looking for the *Donald*. Only once did they see a coast guard cutter. She circled for a while and then went off.

Jim Clark came out several times during these days. He was always accompanied by companions, different each time generally but all of the same sort. One whose name was not mentioned looked the most sinister; tall, cadaverous, middle-aged, he wore a tight suit, ankle boots and a straw hat. He asked that the schooner be brought in to twenty miles off as he had boats ready to shuttle a large quantity of liquor ashore. But the boats never appeared. Usually they threw out hopes for the arrival of the *Donald* suggesting that she would be at a position other than where the *Hazel Herman* happened to be. On one occasion it was the rumour that the *Donald* had been dismasted in the hurricane, losing some of her crew, and had been towed to Havana, which tended to confirm the thought that she had been fully loaded. Such a disaster was not illogical because it was learned that a number of vessels had suffered damage and some had been driven ashore with the loss of all hands.

In spite of conversations on deck, which Captain Pentz was left out of but which looked to him, as viewed from the poop, like deals, with hand-shaking and nods of agreement on the part of the visitors, Bowman Rafuse became increasingly agitated and worried. At one point he was anxious to be taken ashore but was dissuaded by Clark.

Between visits he seemed to want to take his mind off his problems. He tried shooting at bottles thrown over the side with the double-barreled shotgun. It was the only gun on board, as far as Pentz knew, except his own German automatic which he had soberly purchased on the advice of a seemingly knowledgeable acquaintance in Mobile and which he kept in his hip pocket. It was useless though. He had found that the bullets he had bought did not fit it. But the revolver might serve as a bluff.

Gabriel Pentz concluded that everyone was a liar. Oddly enough he again felt sorry for Rafuse. He wanted to help him—and extricate himself too. Someone, he thought, must be double-crossing him.

On Sunday the 9th, when the sun was hardly an hour above the horizon, Captain Pentz sighted a boat, a mere speck, coming out from the coast. Presently he looked at it through the glasses and decided that it was heading in his direction. He called Rafuse who came up from the cabin in his shirt and pants and bare feet.

"Reckon they're making this way," Pentz said. "We might stop and ask them if they've seen the *Donald*."

They had been beating against a light southerly wind during the night watches in their ceaseless search—or that was what Gabriel Pentz understood they were doing. Now he swung the vessel off and moved slowly to the westward to meet the boat. The two seamen who had handled the sails were leaning against the rail. The craft gradually grew larger.

"One of them high-speed launches," Pentz commented.

Rafuse's composure seemed to be shaken again. He did not answer. He walked about the poop with quick steps, stopped, looked at the approaching boat, then moved around in the confined space and strode along the deck—then back.

"Must have left St. Augustine before dawn," Pentz remarked.

"Suppose," Rafuse grunted.

In another ten minutes the boat was within hailing distance. In the silence of their sailing they heard the powerful motor throttle down.

A voice through a megaphone came over the water. "Have you seen a three-masted schooner?"

Captain Pentz answered that he had not. That was what he was looking for. Had they seen the *Donald* anywhere?

There was no reply to this and the launch came closer.

The voice came again. "Man wants to see you, Yeoman. We'll come alongside."

Being partially deaf Rafuse did not catch it all. Pentz repeated it. He hesitated for a moment and then said, "No."

Captain Pentz put his megaphone to his mouth again. "Don't come alongside. Stand off." And he waved them away.

"Seem to be acquainted with you, Bowman."

"They have no business with me. Don't let them aboard."

"Okay."

The boat turned and went astern of the *Hazel Herman*.

Without taking his eyes off the launch Rafuse said, "Where's that gun I was using, Gabe?"

"On the main hatch, far as I know." He took several paces. "Yeah. Lying on the hatch."

The launch came up the port side some way off. Pentz kept his course, moving very slowly through the calm sea.

Now the voice came without the megaphone; it carried well in the stillness of the early morning.

"Like to come aboard, Yeoman. Okay?"

Pentz told him what the voice had said.

"I don't know!" Rafuse exploded in a low tone. "What does he want I wonder?" He swung his body this way and that, staring at the boat and then at the opposite horizon.

"You know the party, Bowman?"

"Not sure."

There was silence for a minute. Then Pentz spoke again.

"Looks like he's pushing on."

The launch was overtaking them, moving up ahead. Then it was given more power, made a wide sweep and came by well off the starboard side. Having made a complete circuit it swung round the stern again and came up on the quarter. The launch's motor chugged slowly now. Pentz counted five men, perhaps six, in the boat.

"Don't seem to want to leave us," Pentz observed.

Bowman Rafuse had been running his fingers through his hair. He let his arm drop to his side. "Oh, better tell him to come aboard," he murmured.

"Friendly?"

"Guess so...Yeah. It's okay."

But Gabriel Pentz hesitated.

Suddenly the launch's engine revved up, the boat lept forward and shot alongside, a roar of stern power arresting its way.

Without warning a man jumped to the schooner's wooden rail. Instantly he pulled a gun from a holster, pointed it at the captain and in a grating yet clear voice said, "Stick 'em up!"

Captain Pentz's mood changed abruptly. A blaze of anger shot through him; less for what was said than the audacity of the boarding.

He recognized the meaning of the order. Yet it sounded absurd, almost funny, corny. Thoughts, like lightning, lept through his mind. Stupid lout standing there saying 'stick 'em up.' They didn't really say that if they meant business. What would they say? He was big, heavy...too heavy to be balancing on the rail...Curiously, he noticed, the man held his gun in his left hand—a fair sized pistol...

The order came again, more urgently.

The distance between the two was about forty feet. Pentz was standing alone on the port side of the cabin trunk. The helmsman had fallen flat to the deck by the wheel. Rafuse had vanished.

So he meant it! but obey him...a stranger?

The captain's right hand went down to his hip pocket. He fumbled a second while he watched the man. Then he saw the flash.

He heard the crack of the pistol and felt something bite his arm—his left arm. He whipped out his dead revolver.

Raising it, he backed up to gain the protection of the cabin companionway. But before he reached it he was shot in the stomach.

The useless gun fell from his hand.

As he crawled down the companionway he heard, as though at a great distance, another shot ring out. Then another one much louder. Crumpling on the deck of his cabin he vaguely sensed that yet another shot had been fired.

When the captain disappeared below the hijacker swung round and shot the cook who had just come on deck from the forecastle. The bullet pierced his collar bone.

But that was his last shot—and almost his last breath.

One of the seamen, known as Richard, had lifted the shotgun from the hatch unnoticed. He aimed and fired quickly. The hijacker was thrown back, toppled and fell overboard. He dropped between the schooner and the launch.

While the echo of the firing reverberated over the water the launch closed the gap.

Suddenly another man was on the rail. He faltered a moment to recover his balance, gun in hand.

The seaman did not wait for him to gain his trim; he pulled the trigger of his second barrel. The man twisted, hovering on the rail. Then someone in the launch caught him.

The engine roared and the boat sheered off.

The two shells fired from the gun were the only two left. Bowman Rafuse had used all the others—why, it was hard to tell.

When Captain Pentz struggled below he did not expect to survive. He was astonished that he did not lose consciousness. When the men hurried down into his cabin his mind was working clearly in spite of his weakness and the pain in his forearm.

He ordered the mate and two men to go back on deck and make as militant an appearance as possible until the launch, which was lying off astern, had made its next move. He had the remaining seaman, Richard, put a tourniquet on his arm, which was bleeding copiously and wrap a sheet around his waist with several turns—the bullet had entered his navel, though it gave him little actual pain.

"Pull it good and tight," he instructed. Richard nearly wrung the life out of him.

The mate returned to report the boat underway at high speed and making for the shore.

"Steer for St. Augustine...course about west-sou'-west." His voice was shaky. "Hoist the distress signal...Catch every breath of wind there is." He paused. "If you see a boat...try to get her to take us in tow...or ship me to...St. Augustine. Harbour's no more'n a gutter...can't get a schooner in." His voice trailed off.

The *Hazel Herman* added her maintopsail to the rest of her canvas but seemed only to idle through the shimmering sea, her wake like the trickle of a stream. Yet her speed was deceptive. At two in the afternoon the mate raised the lighthouse, a needle on a knife-edged horizon. At three a shrimp boat approached in response to the flag of distress.

Pentz, though dazed, heard snatches of one side of an argument in which Rafuse, who was evidently on deck, was trying to persuade a fisherman to engage in an errand of mercy. But the fisherman apparently did not want to become involved in a rum running affair. Presently, however, the man clambered down into the cabin.

As he spoke Pentz said, "You talk like you're a Newfoundlander."

"I am," he answered. "You hail from Lunenburg. That right?"

Pentz said it was.

The response was quick. "Well, I don't care what trouble I get into, I'll take you ashore. Ain't going to leave a Bluenose laying around half dead."

The captain was helped onto the shrimp boat, then the wounded cook and finally Bowman Rafuse jumped aboard. Pentz ordered the mate to shape a course for Jacksonville, go close in and try to get picked up by the coast guard. "Don't run her aground," were his final words.

That was the last Captain Gabriel Pentz saw of the *Hazel E. Herman.*

After scratching a will of sorts on a sheet of paper at the suggestion of a doctor at the Flagler Hospital in St. Augustine, a surgeon pulled out the bullet which was lodged against his backbone, sewed him up and forgot him. Not that the surgeon was heartless, or was less sensitive to rum runners than others; he did not expect him to live out the day.

But Gabriel Pentz did.

This may have been partly due to an old shipmate, Captain John Chapman, a Nova Scotian now living in Jacksonville, who came to his rescue when he heard about him. He saw that he was given the best of the crude attention available.

Bowman Rafuse was concerned too. Yet it was not so much to care for the welfare of his captain that he contrived to procure a room for himself in the hospital, as perhaps to take refuge from the gangsters.

Pentz wrote to his wife—a rather muddled letter—saying that he was in hospital with a broken arm and would be there for some time. "I figure to get out when it mends," he finished.

They cut off the fingers of his left hand; they had become gangrenous. But that was not enough. His hand was taken off.

A week later he coughed and the stitches in his stomach parted like the boltropes of his foresail in the storm. Through his semi-conscious mind he heard the doctor speak of peritonitis to someone close to the bed. Pentz knew the word. He had seen the outcome of peritonitis before. He was bandaged after that; stitching would not hold.

Mrs. Pentz was informed by Captain Chapman. She left her four children and made the long journey to Florida. She hardly recognized him at first. He did not speak. His arm gave him the greatest misery.

One hot morning he heard the black woman scrubbing his floor again. After a while the scrubbing stopped. She was speaking.

"Cap. You pray to the Lord?"

Captain Pentz turned his head a little and opened his eyes. She was not old. Her crisp hair was tied tightly at the back of her velvety neck. He looked beyond and watched a fly moving up the screened window.

"I think I've consulted...the Almighty," he said at last. He felt her observing him intently. "In a manner of speaking," he added.

His eyes returned to the woman. Her black hands rested on her bucket as she knelt. He was attracted by her beauty as she spoke again.

"I know you not goin' to die, Cap, 'cause I'se been prayin' for you."

He closed his eyes again. "Thanks," he murmured. "Thanks."

Presently he found the bed more comfortable. It was quiet, peaceful in the room. Her assertion floated through his mind; he could remember every word she said—or was it really she who said it?

Towards the end of September a man from the Department of Justice came to see Captain Pentz. Mr. Wilcox said he had been told it would have been useless to interview him earlier in the month.

"You're a miracle they say." He was looking down at the man who had so nearly died of wounds, sitting up in a wicker chair. "They don't know what caused you to survive. Salt water and mercurochrome, they tell me, was all they had."

The invalid laughed. "I live by salt water."

The Justice Department's Mr. Wilcox asked Captain Pentz to identify, if he could, photographs of several people. There was Jim Clark and the cadaverous unnamed one whose boats never came, and there was the man he knew as Silver, Steve Metcalf. But the photograph that jolted him when he saw it was that of one, Tom Irwin, according to Wilcox. "They call him Left-handed Dan."

"Yeah," agreed Pentz. "That's the man who shot me. Yeah. He fired with his left hand."

That was all just then but a few days later Mr. Wilcox returned with two men. When brought before him Captain Pentz identified one as the man steering the high-powered launch and the other as the man standing in the bow when the boat came alongside.

Pentz made a brief statement to Wilcox which he signed with a fairly strong hand. In October he was obliged to dictate a much longer account to the Department of Justice and was then asked if he wished to lay a charge against the hijackers.

"No," said Pentz. "Enough damage has been done already. I'm going home with my wife soon."

Then it was that Wilcox seemed to be freed from the obligation of reticence about the crime.

"Probably better to let the matter lay, Captain."

"Well, I don't understand it anyway," Pentz said. "Do you?"

They were sitting on the patio of the hospital under the shade of a green canopy. Gabriel Pentz had paced from one side to the other several times during the morning. The pain in his left arm was still severe but his stomach gave him little trouble. He was eating quite well and had gained much weight since his wife first saw him in his emaciated condition.

"No, I do not claim to understand it fully," Wilcox replied, stretching his legs out before him. "The Justice Department has several conjectures."

"I wouldn't be averse to hearing them."

"This fellow Bowman Rafuse is a gambler, at times a drinker, an imaginative dealer. That's on the bad side. You said he really has a good heart."

"He has, I think."

"That's something." Wilcox studied his perforated shoes. "Rafuse owned the schooner, not the cargo. He had probably collected the freight on it— and on rum freight's mighty high. It seems he conceived the idea of selling the cargo to another rum running syndicate instead of transferring it to the *Donald.* I guess he didn't think far enough when he made the arrangement. By and by he realized he was implicated in a murder scheme and tried to back out, and dispose of the rum before the syndicate came out for it. But neither he nor you could find the *Donald* and no one helped you to find her. He was being double-crossed by his own agents."

"That's not hard for me to picture," Pentz observed.

"He didn't mind too much if he lost the *Hazel Herman.* She was insured. But there was you—-and the crew. Yet he had provided himself with a black crew. He was geared for easy disposal there."

"I sometimes wondered..." Pentz murmured.

"When Bowman Rafuse reneged on the deal the party with whom he made it decided to hijack the rum. To make quite sure the job would be carried out successfully they hired this Left-handed Dan from New York. They wouldn't have employed that type of hardened gangster if they hadn't meant rough business, the complete business. As you may know these liquor syndicates have their headquarters in New York mostly; some are in Boston, some in Montreal."

"I wasn't acquainted with the fact," Pentz remarked.

"Their plan was not unlike others that have taken place on the coast. The advance party was to shoot up the master and crew, then craft would come out to unload, and after that the schooner scuttled or set afire."

"Oh!" exclaimed Pentz shortly.

"Maybe Rafuse would have escaped death."

"He was a mighty scared man them last days."

"No doubt."

"Maybe that's why he left two shots in the gun. He seemed to want to get rid of them earlier on."

"No doubt," Wilcox said again.

"If I'd have put my hands up I'd have been worse off eventually," Pentz suggested, raising his eyebrows.

"I suppose so. *You'd* have been twenty fathoms down instead of Left-handed Dan. I don't think they expected resistance."

"And the other guy that the seaman shot?"

"He was brought into this same hospital a while before you and your injured cook arrived. That's how we got a line on the gangsters."

"Oh," said Pentz.

"He, like your cook, was patched up pretty quickly."

The captain pondered a while. "Richard. Fine man, Richard. Good hand, too. Was a soldier at one time, he told me. Saved my life—all our lives."

"He sure did."

Pentz knocked the dottle out of his pipe. "You going to take the case any further?" he asked.

Wilcox shook his head. "You're going back to Canada aren't you?"

"Yes."

Captain Gabriel Pentz exerted double pressure with his right arm and eased himself out of the chair. He walked slowly to the edge of the patio, looked across towards the harbour that was 'no more than a gutter' and came back.

"Where's the *Hazel Herman?*"

"Don't know. Gone, I guess. Disappeared."

The Perilous Channel

The motor fishing vessel *Viking Warrior* left Folkestone soon after three in the morning and headed out into the English Channel. After running seven miles through the inshore traffic zone she reached her grounds in the west-going shipping lane of the Strait of Dover. She let down her nets and began to trawl in the cold mid-winter darkness.

Her skipper, Valentine Noakes, checked his bearings. He could distinguish the flashing lights of buoys marking the Varne Bank and he noticed the navigation lights of two outward bound ships approaching. Presently they passed and others came into sight going the same way. It was a busy thoroughfare. Then, strangely, a ship was seen coming up-channel out of the thin mist making for the North Sea.

She passed the *Viking Warrior* about four o'clock, her hull standing out clearly against the thinly clouded moonlit sky. Noakes shook his head. "Some still go the wrong way." he grumbled to the man tending the trawl. "Foreigner likely." He shrugged his shoulders. "Well, none of our business." But he did not like it because he ought only to have to concern himself with ships coming in one direction. Noakes had observed ships doing this before though seldom since I.M.C.O., the International Maritime Consultative Organization, had recommended the dual-highway system in 1966 whereby west-bound traffic kept to the English side of the Strait and the east-bound to the French side. No law, however, compelled this.

Noakes went on fishing, the trawler riding the breaking sea easily. Suddenly he was startled by the sound of a deep explosion rumbling over the water. Seconds later came a concussion. The shock seemed to stop the *Viking Warrior* in her slow progress as though she wanted to wait and listen.

Valentine Noakes saw nothing though he strained to discern a flare. But the direction of the sound was certain, up-channel; not from ashore. It was born of the sea; he knew that. It could not be far. A ship: what else?

The roar of the explosion died away but still sang in his ears.

The fisherman, with a lifelong experience of the most crowded strait in the world, stayed a moment longer, then jumped to his radio. He called North Foreland and spoke over the static. "Vessel exploded approximately two miles west of the Varne Bank. Proceeding." The message was timed 4:10 a.m. on January 11, 1971.

The crew of the *Viking Warrior* hauled their nets and Skipper Noakes steered for the position from which the sound had come. His course was true. In ten minutes a shadow evolved ahead of him and, in the luminous night, quickly shaped itself into the profile of a ship, a tanker by its bulky mould, lying stopped broadside to the tide.

Coming close up under her stern which stood high above him, the four blades of her propeller clear of the water and her rudder aport, he read the words beneath her taffrail, *Texaco Caribbean*. Swinging round and moving up abreast of her he found the hull ended near her foremast.

Her bow was gone.

Noakes hailed the deck several times but there was no reply.

At 7:25 a.m. North Foreland received yet another terse message, this time from a ship naming herself *Paracas*: "Position Latitude 51° North, Longitude 01° 20' East. Collision."

The operator at the principal radio station in the Dover Strait now knew enough to announce the calamity, though only vaguely, to ships in the vicinity. The Dover and Dungeness lifeboat stations were notified as well and the coast-guard establishment at Deal, midway between North Foreland and Dover.

But people along part of the nearby English coast were already aware of it. Windows had rattled and many broke in Folkestone. Alarm struck residents of Sandgate eight miles from the eruption, for fear of another cliff-slide or land movement along the already unstable earth fault. Yet Lightsman Wild, senior hand on the *Varne* light vessel neither saw nor heard anything during the early morning hours though only four and one-half miles away. But he was up wind and the visibility was poor.

At Dover, as at other strategic ports, a salvage tug lay at her wharf, idle yet alert. It was the business of the deep-sea German tug *Heros* to wait and listen—in expectation of a commercial venture rather more than a mission of mercy. She left the harbour with the utmost dispatch; and at about that time the Dover lifeboat was launched.

In response to the radio message ships coming through the strait slowed down in readiness to assist the stricken ones. The Norwegian *Bravour* moved cautiously. The tanker *Stella Antares* reported that she was searching. A few minutes later the *Bravour* said she was passing the stern section of the *Texaco Caribbean* and could see no evidence of life on board. She spoke of a ship she named *Paracas* still afloat but gave no further information about her.

Presently the *Bravour* signalled that she had picked up nineteen men of the *Texaco Caribbean*, though she did not say from what, a boat or the water. Then the *Viking Warrior* announced that she was near ships searching and had "one man on board who requires an ambulance at Folkestone Pier in half an hour."

The Dover lifeboat took the nineteen men from the *Bravour* so that she could continue her voyage, and having plucked from the sea two more set out for Dover which she reached at seven o'clock. The coast-guard at Deal learned that there were nine members of the crew of the *Texaco Caribbean* still missing. By 6:15 a.m. the two or three other ships who had stopped that morning had resumed their journeys leaving the Dungeness lifeboat and a tug, the *Diligent*, whose interest was natural to her calling, searching the neighbourhood. As daylight appeared an R.A.F. plane joined the hunt for survivors.

The tug *Heros* found the *Paracas* quickly in spite of the mist. She was at anchor half a mile from the tanker she had rammed. When the tug captain saw her battered bow he wondered how the anchor could have been free enough to dislodge itself. He wasted no time in offering assistance to the large freighter—the first tug on the scene had the prior claim if he could persuade the wounded ship to accept his services. He provided portable pumps at once and climbed aboard himself with a salvage agreement in his pocket and inspected the damage with the somewhat distraught master of the vessel.

Her bow was pushed back, her forecastle ripped and crushed, her windlass destroyed. Her fore peak tank and forward hold were taking water. Amazingly no lives had been lost.

The tug captain disembarked with Lloyd's Open Form of Salvage Agreement duly signed by Captain Anacama, Master of the Peruvian motor vessel. He made his long heavy hawser fast to the stern, the ship slipped her cable and let it sink, and just after eight o'clock as dawn broke the tug got underway towing the *Paracas* stern first, destined for Hamburg.

The *Paracas*, of 9,500 tons, was bound from Peru to the ports of Brake on the Weser and Hamburg with a cargo of fish oil and fishmeal. She was well found and had traded to Europe before. Why Captain Anacama chose to keep to the left up the English Channel against the recommendations of the international authority was not known, though he was not unique in this behavior among shipmasters of far countries. He may have elected to be guided by the lighthouses of England in preference to those of France, the former being better, but once on the wrong side it was difficult to cross over. Or he may just have been unaware of the one-way system. He must have encountered a great deal of traffic coming towards him. He could have taken a pilot but the economics of some traders prohibited their use where not compulsory. Moreover, a captain was supposed to know his way in the open sea however congested—and mid-channel was the open sea.

Now, for his navigational sins, which every master must risk in foreign waters, he had to travel ignominiously backwards for the rest of his voyage.

The *Texaco Caribbean* was not a supertanker but still a large vessel, 13,604 gross tons and capable of carrying 20,000 tons of oil. She sailed as a Panamanian and was owned by Texaco Panama Inc., a foreign flag subsidiary of the American oil company. Commanded by thirty-nine-year old Captain Franko Giurini, she was manned by a crew of thirty-four Italians. She had discharged her cargo of gas oil and petro-chemicals at the ports of London and Terneuzen and was now on her way back to Trinidad in ballast, her tanks being one-third filled with sea water.

Captain Giurini had discussed the trim of his ship and her ballasting with his chief officer while steaming out of the estuary of the Wester Schelde the evening before and had decided to follow the usual practice of filling the tanks sufficiently to provide a good grip of the water on her winter voyage across the Atlantic while keeping the ship light enough to make an economicl passage. They would clean their tanks when they were well past the Azores. This meant that in the meantime she would have a small residue of her old cargo still in her tanks creating a gaseous vapour which might not be fully ventilated.

The night was not clear enough for Captain Giurini to see the South Goodwin light-vessel when he came up from his cabin to join the second officer on the bridge as they approached the English coast, but their navigational devices told them where they were until they entered the west-going track through the Strait of Dover.

He observed the hazy lights of several other ships going with him into the four-mile wide ocean-going shipping lane. The Varne lightship, which marked the near end of the long slim bank which divided the lane into two still narrower passages, soon appeared to port and slipped by. Ten minutes elapsed. Then, to his surprise, he saw through the mist the masthead lights of a vessel coming towards him.

The lookoutman in the crowsnest hailed her approach; the officer-of-the-watch uttered a cry.

In a moment both green and red sidelights came into view, blurred and spongy but, as quickly, focussed clear and bright enough to appear perilously threatening.

Giurini ordered the wheel thrown hard astarboard. The steam whistle blared with a single blast.

In a patch of moonlight sweeping the sea the black hull of the on-coming vessel suddenly became large and near. The breaking curve of her phosphorescent bow-wave glistened white and spangled. She stood on as though unmanned.

The tanker's response to her rudder was slow. In desperation the captain shouted to put the engines full astern.

But it was too late. The sound of the crash was obliterated by the explosion.

Captain Edward Lawrence was reading the Monday morning paper while having his breakfast. It was still dark outside. The telephone rang. The caller urgently relayed a message that had just come in to the Trinity House Corporation's depot at Harwich from the coast-guard. It told of the collision and such facts as were known up to that time, and in particular the danger to navigation which the derelict and its sunken bow seemed to present.

The superintendent of the depot nearest the Strait absorbed the information as quickly as he would otherwise have swallowed his forsaken coffee. He told the duty officer on the telephone to instruct the captain of the tender *Siren* to load two wreck buoys and proceed at once to the general position indicated, there to locate the sunken danger and mark it.

The authority for England's lighthouses and offshore marks had rested with Trinity House for almost 500 years and this august body took its responsibility for the safe navigation of ships through its waters and certain regions beyond with the steady zeal born of royal assent. It readily ventured outside its territorial limits when risk to shipping threatened; and this was gratefully acknowledged by France and her neighbouring North Sea countries. The area of the Varne Bank was beyond England's maritime boundary; but a wreck in that narrow sea could not go unmarked where 700 ships took passage every day. Trinity House would establish the warning.

The broken hull of the *Texaco Caribbean* was one of those cases, and the lighthouse tender *Siren*, Commander Adrian Burnell, sailed out of Harwich at 9:35 that morning to indicate its position. When he reached the South Foreland south of the Goodwin Sands, Burnell came upon an oil slick and since the tide was flooding he followed it.

In the early afternoon he was informed that the stern half of the ship had sunk. And now the search for the eight missing men, including Captain Giurini, had been given up.

The *Siren* arrived at the end of the slick as daylight was failing. It was roughly the position where the wreck had been reported. Commander Burnell, a master mariner with the experience of forty years at sea and two years commanding the *Siren* in her exacting and sensitive work, anchored close to the rising oil and launched his two motor boats in the slackening tide. They swept to a considerable depth and snagged an object but the sweep slid over it and they could not tell what it was. The boats had to return at six o'clock because of darkness and were hoisted in until morning.

The tender then took on the duties of a wreck-marking vessel by exhibiting three green lights vertically from her foremast, signifying that ships must pass to the westward of her, the side away from the Varne Shoal. Commander Burnell considered his vessel to be anchored in a position three cables west of the wreck, though which section he did not know, he hoped both (which in fact was the case).

A general radio warning had been transmitted at 3:26 p.m. and was broadcast at intervals thereafter until nine o'clock that night.

The *Paracas* was now in the North Sea off the Belgian coast in tow of the *Heros* and another salvage tug which had put on board additional pumps. The battered ship's progress towards Hamburg was satisfactory.

At this hour the German Hapag-Lloyd motor vessel *Brandenburg* was leaving her dock at Antwerp bound for Puerto Rico, fully loaded with 4,000 tons of cargo—cars, cement, crated household goods. Though twenty years old she was a sturdy ship with a crew of twenty-nine men, mostly Spaniards, and two women.

Her master, Captain Peter Rahman, thirty-five, remained on the bridge with the river pilot throughout the passage down the winding Schelde. During the day he had heard over the radio in his cabin something about a serious collision in the English Channel and he asked the pilot if he knew anything about it. The pilot had heard nothing.

The *Texaco Caribbean* sinks after colliding with the *Paracas*. Inset map shows the routes of the doomed vessels in the English Channel.

Radio Officer Timm brought a weather report up to the captain at nine o'clock. He had just received it from Scheveningen, the radio station they favoured for weather because of its detail. Rahman asked Timm if he had heard any messages about a tanker accident in the Channel. He had not. He then instructed him to watch for such a warning. Soon Timm returned to the radio room, but caught no word of it before he went off duty.

At 2:30 on the morning of January 12, the pilot was disembarked at the mouth of the river and at four o'clock the first officer, Peter Trelle, came on watch when the *Brandenburg* was off the West Hinder. Three hours later she entered the Strait. The ship slipped smoothly along on a dying ebb tide at fourteen knots, a gentle southerly breeze rippling the sea and making the wavelets glint in the pale yellow track of the low full moon. The air was cold and crisp.

Approaching the Varne Bank Trelle observed a hazy green light some distance away on the starboard bow, but through his binoculars it transformed itself into three green superimposed lights. The radar showed them to belong to a fairly large stationary vessel and the *Brandenburg* would clear her easily to starboard. He also saw the lights of a fisherman moving slowly beyond. He held his course and speed. The captain had gone below to his cabin ten minutes before, having been on the bridge all night, and Trelle had no wish to bring him up again merely to confirm the presence of a wreck-marker. He was pretty confident in his mind that the number and position of the lights were meant to warn ships that they were to be passed on the mariner's starboard hand.

The *Siren* was abeam at about 7:30 at a distance of just over half a mile according to Trelle's observations. He recognized her dim form to be a temporary light-ship—she had no tower.

Two minutes passed; then three.

Suddenly Trelle was thrown against the fore part of the bridge. The helmsman's body came hard against the wheel.

A heavy, lurching shock was transmitted through the ship. No one on board would have failed to feel the forward motion of the laden hull being jerkily restrained.

Trelle had almost to push himself from the bridge rail. He heard a hissing noise somewhere on the port quarter. Rather than turning around to question it he instinctively looked ahead. His line of vision dropped from the sea beyond to the bow of the ship. It was low in the water, as though descending into a trough of a wave.

He shouted to the officer cadet who was on watch with him. "Get everyone up—we're sinking."

Captain Rahman was beside him. "What's happened?" he asked breathlessly.

"I don't know. The ship's going down... Struck something. Hit something submerged... She's not aground, that's certain."

Rahman tried to take the way off his ship with the engines. He told Trelle to sound the horn on the funnel, but before the first officer had completed the distress signal it apparently ran out of compressed air.

Hands were clambering on deck. The bos'un was ordered to lower the port lifeboat—the ship had begun to list to starboard.

Trelle leapt to the radar, identified the Varne light-vessel and, with practiced skill, read its bearing and distance, 045°, 5.4 miles. He glanced at the clock; it was 7:35. Gasping the UHF telephone he pressed the grip to tell of their plight. It was dead.

Captain Rahman then left the bridge and went to the boat deck to direct the abandonment of the ship.

The *Brandenburg* was listing more steeply. Outside Trelle glanced down at the fore deck. The bow had disappeared; the deck was under water back to No. 2 hatch, the sea breaking against the foot of the foremast—she was still underway, heading downwards.

The *Brandenburg* was now heeling to such a degree that the big lifeboat could be lowered no further. The bos'un left it and ran to assist the third officer in disengaging the two self-inflating rafts on the after deck. They accomplished no more than knocking out the securing shackles of one of them and throwing off its gripes. But others had been released by the seamen. They had to jump clear of the water swirling over the rail. They climbed to the boat deck.

Those who came from the accommodation did so blindly not understanding the predicament, seeing little at first but sensing an unnatural state, the strange dark lopsided condition, encountering water where it should not be. Soon they knew they should have brought their lifebelts. Those who had been on deck, and most had been because the watches were about to change, had no time to go back for life preservers. The captain grabbed a few from a locker and threw them among the men.

But at that moment the boat deck, angled to starboard with the increasing list, submerged.

Almost grotesquely the after end of the deck came up again and spilled the risen water. The bow must have struck the bottom and up-ended the stern—the ship was four times longer than the depth of the sea. Then it lowered itself and sank.

All hands were in the water except those trapped below.

The usual loose material lying on deck after leaving port floated off and served to support some of the crew, but there was little enough. Both Rahman and Trelle encouraged the crew to keep together and not to lose heart. Trelle called out that the wreck-marking vessel was sure to have seen their ship going down and would rescue them within twenty minutes. How much the Spaniards understood was uncertain.

Those who found nothing to cling to lasted but a short time: the water was very cold.

A few ships were in sight but the foundering of the *Brandenburg* had passed unnoticed. Even the wreck-marking tender, less than a mile away, seemed to remain unconscious of the disaster.

Skipper Valentine Noakes cast off his lines from the quay at Folkestone at four o'clock, only an hour later than he had the morning before when he had discovered the first crippled ship. Among other fishermen who were going out with him was the *Whitby Rose*. Noakes took his *Viking Warrior* to his usual grounds off the Varne Bank. He saw the three green lights two or three miles to the east of him and knew they would be carried by a Trinity House tender marking the wreck.

While it was still dark, having remained in the area trawling, he saw a small light about one and one-half miles away.

"Probably a buoy laid by the tender," he observed to his mate. He took no further notice of it until dawn faintly lightened the sea. Then Noakes saw it was a boat. Three men seemed to be standing up in the craft; they were waving.

"Work boat from the tender," he speculated. "Catching fish for the crew's breakfast, no doubt. Waving to tell us they're in the same business as us." He turned his attention to his own trawling.

But the *Whitby Rose* was closer to the object and her skipper saw they were not fishing. Nor was it a boat. It was a raft.

The *Whitby Rose* picked up the wet, shivering men and immediately sent a message of distress. Her skipper also told Noakes what he had found. The *Viking Warrior* hurried to the rescue, also notifying the radio station of the apparent situation.

Listening to the chatter of the various fishermen on the ship-to-shore radio frequency, Mrs. Serena Fair in Folkestone, who had been an official watcher on behalf of the National Lifeboat Service for fifty years, heard the conversation between the two trawlers and telephoned the coxswain of the Dungeness lifeboat. He knew nothing about a casualty and telephoned the coast-guard. Within minutes the coxswain fired his maroons to summon the crew and quickly launched his boat.

The *Viking Warrior* pulled five men from the water, three supported by a crate, among them Trelle, and two clinging to a piece of timber. One was already dead.

Having hauled his nets Noakes searched for almost an hour after that but finding no other survivors he made for Folkestone. One other fisherman picked up five men and retrieved five bodies.

No boat had come from the *Siren*.

The search, as the catastrophe became known, was joined by several ships in the vicinity as well as by helicopters, but no one else was found.

The final count that day was eleven rescued, six drowned; one dead in hospital, and thirteen still missing, including the captain, the radio officer and the two stewardesses.

On Tuesday morning, January 12, the anchor watch on board the *Siren* from four to eight o'clock was kept by Quartermaster Smith, a man of many years experience on Trinity House tenders. His station was on the bridge, his principal task being to see that ships coming down the Channel did not run over the wreck ground—assuming his warnings would keep them away— and also did not pass between his vessel and the Varne Bank a mile or so from her, this being considered an uncertain reach. Should any ship attempt to do so he was to flash danger signals from a hand lamp when the ship was yet two miles away. At closer range he would blow warning signals or the whistle.

Visibility was about four miles but the quartermaster did not have to depend on his eyes alone, he had the radar. The instrument was set to provide a large display of objects within three miles, and had a range-marker which produced a warning sound when a ship came within half a mile.

Throughout his watch Smith saw many ships go by on the port side— the vessel was lying to her anchor on the last half of the ebb tide. He checked about twenty of them on the radar. None passed on the wrong side, towards the Varne, though he knew some had earlier in the night. He left the bridge for a few minutes at 6:45 to call the crew and again at 7:15 to call his relief. Before going below he made sure nothing was approaching the danger zone. He returned the second time at about 7:18. He glanced around and saw no steaming lights approaching the forbidden area, nor any blips in that region on the radar screen. Being satisfied all was clear he entered the weather conditions in the log book, went into the radio room abaft the wheelhouse and recorded the messages in the signal log, then wound the three clocks, the last being in the wheelhouse.

It was quiet on the bridge, just the ticking of instruments; the wind was light and made no whine. The six windows across the front of the wheelhouse were shut but the doors at either side were wide open. He could occasionally hear work going on on deck; the boats were being made ready to resume sweeping.

Before the end of his watch he was out on the port wing of the bridge observing two ships passing. As he turned round to come back, he noticed a small flashing light astern apparently a mile or two away down-channel. He could not understand it. Just then the captain came up; he had seen it too.

The two motor boats were being lowered. When about to leave Commander Burnell ordered the coxswain of one of them to investigate the source of the light. It turned out to be a life-raft with an automatic light. It was brought alongside and on examination was found to have German markings on it. Burnell and his officers concluded that it was probably from the *Texaco Caribbean* as she had traded with Germany.

The boats carried on sounding and sweeping in this vicinity and soon found a wreck. Having determined its extent the *Siren* moved and buoyed it.

It was ten o'clock by now and the radio officer had just intercepted a message from the Folkestone pilot station informing pilots of the sinking of a ship that morning just where the *Siren* lay. Astounded by this news Burnell made an immediate inquiry and learned something of the fate of the *Brandenburg*. He discovered that he had probably already marked the German freighter unknowingly. Since a number of boats and aircraft were searching for survivors, and since his vessel had to remain stationary, he decided to continue with his urgent charge. His boats therefore swept where they had given up the previous afternoon when darkness fell. This led to the finding of one section of the *Texaco Caribbean* by noon, which was duly buoyed, and the other beneath a tidal turbulance by mid-afternoon.

At nightfall the *Siren* again acted as the wreck-marking vessel with a series of buoys exhibiting green flashing lights around the outskirts of the wrecks.

The next day a number of vessels were sent to the scene to examine the sunken hulks for salvage possibilities. Three more Trinity House tenders came; Risdon Beazley's salvage vessel *Queen Mother* sent divers down; Smit & Company's Dutch salvage tug *Orca* arrived on contract for the owners of *Brandenburg*. HMS *Lowestoft* sounded with sonar; there was a pilot boat with an echo sounder; a cable ship; and none other than the omnipresent *Viking Warrior* chartered as a diving boat by the Folkestone Salvage Company. By the 15th *Number 6* light-vessel took up a position north-east of the wrecks, up-channel, in the direction from which ships approached.

During this period and henceforward frequent warnings were issued to ships outward bound from British and European north sea ports. Notwithstanding this ships came perilously close to the danger zone and some steamed through it disregarding all signals.

Conditions for diving were favourable at first, the sea was quiet. But descent was limited to thirty minutes at high and low water—the flow was too swift to go down in the five hours or so in between.

The sea floor at this point in the Channel had a depth of eighty feet at low water; about one hundred feet at the top of the tide. It was more or less level and sandy, sprinkled with shells and small stones. Visibility below in calms was good.

Soundings had established the amount of water over the wrecks, expressed for safety's sake in terms of low tide. The bow section of the *Texaco Caribbean*, one hundred and twenty feet in length from its stem to the jagged plating where it had been severed in the blast, was at a depth of twenty-three feet. The main part of the hull, a quarter of a mile to the south-east, had only four feet of water over it.

This part of the long tanker lay silently on her starboard side as though she had just fallen over. The wreck almost fitted the depth of the sea—her beam being seventy-eight feet. Her bridge was missing. But it was presently discovered not far from the bow, still attached to the boat deck on which stood boatless davits.

Her name on the stern was plain to see underwater. But above the T of Texaco a great swath had been cut through the side plating from the port quarter of the poop almost to the bilge. The steel was clean and bright where the paint had been shaved off and the framework ahead of the propeller had been ripped out, like the insides of a gored animal, and was suspended above the cavity.

The *Brandenburg* had evidently hit the end of the tanker and cut her way through it. Had her course taken her one hundred feet south she would have escaped. After striking she forged on for half a mile while sliding to the bottom.

Divers found a hole torn one hundred feet along the port bilge of the *Brandenburg* which opened Nos. 1 and 2 holds to the sea. Her bottom and even her heavy flat keel were buckled. As the sea flooded into the two forward holds she had listed to the side where the water could not free itself. When her bow struck the hard sand she must have pivoted and swung to the last of the ebb heading north-east, as though she wanted to return to her home port. As she settled on the sand she turned over on her starboard side, the heavier side, her masts and funnel going under.

Immediately after their preliminary descent on the *Brandenburg* divers were instructed to extricate any bodies of missing crewmen who might have been trapped in the ship as she sank. They felt their way along the now vertical decks and entered the accommodation by the passageways. Where cabin doors were open they got in but found no one; those that were closed could not be opened—they had swollen and jammed. It was too dangerous to attempt to gain entry by the portholes. Life within, if there had been any, had almost certainly been extinguished.

It was not long before a swell rutted the sea and as it grew it became murky below and hindered the men. It was a slow business. Yet time was important in order to confirm the extent of the foul ground and to find a means of clearing the narrow channel through which hundreds of ships passed.

By the 18th they had plugged the gooseneck vents of the *Texaco Caribbean's* bunker oil tanks and so stopped the slow leak and ended the slick which the *Siren* had followed to find the wreck. About 1,000 tons had escaped altogether from both ships but it had not damaged the English or Continental coasts. Some of it still in the bunkers had solidified into a glutinous mass.

During the next six weeks mid-winter gales pounded ships in that great street of water; fog often shrouded the sea forcing freighters and tankers to slow down, and those outward bound through the Strait to listen intently for the piercing blasts of the light-vessel's diaphone. Rain and snow came and long moonless nights, and often the salvage ships lay inactive in the rough seas.

The bodies of three of the missing seamen of the *Texaco Caribbean* were found in her midships accommodation. The body of the master, Captain Franko Giurini, was washed ashore at Sandwich on the Kent coast twelve days after he had lost his ship. He was identified by his widow by a ring on his finger. The three men still missing were never found.

As to the *Paracas*, she was in Hamburg discharging her fish oil and being examined preparatory to going to Bremerhaven for extensive repairs to her bow. There was no way under law by which Britain or any country but her own could bring the *Paracas* under inquiry; no means by which her master could be subpoenaed in a foreign land as a result of a collision in non-territorial waters, nor could her log book come under scrutiny. The centre of the English Channel was looked upon as the 'High Seas.' It would have been different had the accident occurred within three miles of England instead of seven. But no doubt Peru would want to examine the behavior of their ship and her liability.

Restraining ships from entering the restricted square mile was a continuing task for Trinity House. Within the buoyed area the numerous work boats were obvious to on-coming ships by day, their lighted presence on clear nights not unnoticeable; yet ships had constantly to be diverted. The light-vessel guarding the approach had to use a variety of signals to turn them aside, the last in her quiver being a rocket which left with a stunning blast and brilliant light and threw a stream of tracer towards the offender.

Those who seemed to be unaware of the restricted passage were ships of foreign flags, usually of distant nations, masters who were probably unfamiliar with the languages in which the wreck notices were published.

By the end of February some forty ships had been warned off but some had threaded their way through the array of marks.

Then one more paid the price of ignorance.

Lightsman Read and Seaman Banks were keeping the first watch on *Number 6* light-vessel on the night of February 27. *Number 6* was moored as she had been for weeks just ahead of the cockpit of wreckage. On either side of her but a little farther back were two of the green-lighted wreck buoys and in a straight line behind them, at the extremity, were two other buoys with a central one farther back still. Together they made a rhomboid formation and all had radar reflectors. Ships could pass down either side of the complex and were bidden to do so by the two green lights one above the other on each yard-arm of *Number 6*.

The two men followed the approach of every ship bound out through the Strait, and there were many. The procession almost became monotonous until two were suddenly recognized to be coming straight for the light-vessel. It was not uncommon; they had diverted many from the direct approach. But these two held their course in spite of Read's signal on his Aldis handlamp.

He flashed 'U' at short intervals—the international signal 'You are standing into danger.'

No notice was taken.

"Blast their guts," growled Read.

"Keep on," Banks urged. "There's time yet. They'll notice."

The night was clear but very dark, the wind light, the tide running at full ebb.

The masthead lights of the first ship were almost in line a mile or so away. The second seemed to be following closely in her wake.

Read lowered his lamp from his eye for a moment to look more closely "Persistent idiots! Are they blind?"

"There's another coming down!" Banks announced with concern in his voice.

A third ship a little to port of the others and somewhat astern was on a similar course as though following the leader.

The minutes slipped by and still they came on. Read continued flashing.

Seaman Banks waited no longer; he called the captain, then seized the lanyard of the rocket.

As Captain Robinson reached the upper bridge of his light-vessel the flash of the rocket had dissipated but its blast lingered in his head like a clap of thunder. A mass of lighted tracer shot up in an outward trajectory as though from a hose.

The low black hull of the first ship, a dim vision against the night darkness, raced by on the tide close to starboard. She showed no lights but those for navigation. Read was following her with his eye to the sight of his lamp passing his urgent message.

"Leave her," shouted Robinson. "Signal the next ship. U. Quick."

Read swung round and applied his finger to the trigger of the Aldis.

She was nearly on them. As she swept past, so close that her bow wave rocked the light-vessel, a long flash came from the lamp on her bridge indicating acknowledgement of the danger signals.

With her wheel obviously hard over, she swung to starboard under the stern of *Number 6* and steamed out of the area and around the nearest buoy to resume her course outside the perimeter of the domain.

The third ship must have seen the tracer for she turned to port before she reached the light-vessel and went down the Varne side of the channel skirting the buoys.

Captain Robinson hardly waited to assure himself of the safe courses taken by the last two ships before his attention became riveted to the first who was running down the centre. He had caught a change in her track— her green light had appeared but only momentarily. She had turned to starboard but then, as though hesitant of the move, drew back. Soon he could no longer see her stern light.

"Watch there!" Robinson shouted as he jumped down the ladder.

Below at his radio he quickly called the Deal coast-guard and reported a ship having entered the danger zone. "May get through but can't tell yet."

As he hung up and switched over a voice from the bridge cried, "Searchlight astern."

Coming up he did indeed see a powerful searchlight; it was sweeping the water and shining aloft about a mile away near the south-west buoy. Then he saw the navigation lights of the ship from which it came showing her turning and evidently reversing her course—coming up-channel against the traffic. She did not seem to make progress, however.

Leaving Lightsman Read to observe her manoeuvres and Banks to watch other approaching vessels, Captain Robinson slid down the ladder again hardly touching the rungs and grabbed the radio transmitter to inform the coast-guard further. But he had left the instrument tuned to the distress frequency. Before he could change over to the working frequency he heard a conversation in a foreign language, followed by a brief statement in English to the North Foreland radio station, the speaker saying that he thought he had seen a ship sinking west of the Varne and men in the water. He said he was using a searchlight to look and guide other ships to the spot. He added his ship was the Norwegian *Hebris*.

It was 9:12 p.m., about ten minutes since the two ships had passed the light-vessel.

At 9:16 the *Hebris* reported she could not see the ship she thought was sinking. North Foreland retransmitted this signal. Within the next twenty minutes three outbound ships responded saying they were near the mid-Varne buoy or the wreck-markers and were searching.

Robinson could not join the search except as a radio link; *Number 6* had no means of propulsion. She only had two small rowing boats intended exclusively for the safety of the crew and of no use in rescue operations. Men who might have been in the water if not already picked up would have been swept by the ebb tide in the other direction; so there was no point watching over the side.

The motor tanker *Hebris*, which appeared to have been the ship that had swung around the stern of the light-vessel, reported at 10:40 that she had found nothing. Nor had any other ship. But the Dungeness and Dover lifeboats were being launched.

The Dungeness boat came into the Channel well down-stream, at a point about four miles from where the sinking was assumed to have taken place. Travelling against the tide she suddenly came upon a red life-buoy. On hauling it aboard her crew found the name, MS *Niki*, stencilled on it and below it the port of registry, Piraeus. She then encountered loose flotsam, as did the Dover boat which had already found a body on a raft. A Shackleton aircraft illuminated the search area which enabled the two lifeboats to pick up eight bodies, one a woman. A watch found on one had stopped at 9:08. By the morning ten dead had been recovered.

Soon after 8 a.m. the ubiquitous *Viking Warrior* discovered the top of a yellow mast sticking out of the sea and fuel oil coming up around it. At about the same time, as daylight spread across the vexed waters, the master of *Number 6* light-vessel also saw the mast through his binoculars. The Trinity House *Vestal* confirmed that it was attached to a ship sitting upright on the bottom. The mast rose sixteen feet above the surface at low water and would be covered at high water. She buoyed it.

The *Niki* was a small Greek motor cargo vessel of 2,370 tons, 292 feet in length. She was owned by S. Condas Son & Company of Piraeus and was on time charter to Oost Atlantic Lijn, Antwerp. She loaded steel rails in Dunkirk and passed out through the lock at 4:30 p.m. on her last day of life, leaving behind one man in hospital at Le Havre. She spent some time in the roads adjusting her magnetic compasses because of the influence of the steel cargo, then dropped her pilot and sailed for Alexandria.

It was strange that her master, Captain Elias Kampitsis, an experienced seaman of forty-nine, who had steamed through the Strait several times recently, should have allowed his ship to enter the danger zone.

She struck the hidden high stern section of the *Texaco Caribbean* and, being burdened with a dense cargo of steel which left much empty space in her holds, she filled and dived without hesitation. The sea closed over her before anyone had a chance to raise a cry for help. She took the bottom 150 yards from the wreck she hit in perhaps a minute, without stopping.

All hands were lost: the captain, a crew of twenty and the chief engineer's wife. Only the man in Le Havre escaped.

The coroner at the Dover inquest into the death of the crew concluded that "...there was an effective warning system in operation, and it was ignored. When it was realized that *Niki* was in difficulties no effort was spared to rescue her crew."

It was perhaps ironical that at this time Germany expressed its appreciation of the earlier case. The owners of the *Brandenburg* presented thirteen local fishermen who took part in the rescue of the survivors of their ship with inscribed silver watches and 'a book' from the Senate of Hamburg.

The immediate response to the latest tragedy by Trinity House was to lay more buoys, though there should have been no need—the area was unaltered, the *Niki* within it. In all, fourteen buoys encompassed the wrecks, and a week later another light-vessel was added. No one had know such a small circle of open sea so inundated with buoys. Yet ships still tried to get through—and did.

On March 10 the Elder Brethren of Trinity House decided that the three ships were to be dispersed. Risdon Beazley Ullrich Harms was awarded the contract in which they undertook to reduce the wrecks with small cutting charges which would not disturb lights on buoys or passing ships or be heard by the residents of Sandgate. Some wreckage would be removed, some dropped on the sea bed. (It took a year and a half and was the most costly demolition Trinity House had ever had to bear.)

Several aspects of the collisions were not fully answered. Apart from the behavior of the *Paracas*, whose captain may have considered picking up a pilot at Folkestone and then changed his mind and tried to cross over to the up-channel passage off the French coast, the principal questions were: Why did First Officer Trelle of the *Brandenburg* believe he was passing the tender *Siren* on the safe side when he was not? And why did the *Siren* not see the ship or hear her horn? Why did the *Niki* so imprudently stand into obvious danger?

The official inquiry held in Hamburg into the loss of the *Brandenburg* revealed that the first officer knew the meaning of the three green lights as his ship approached the wreck-marking *Siren*. He knew that he must pass the wreck-marker on his starboard side, and he did so, giving her a berth of more than half a mile. But Trelle failed to remember, or realize, that this rule applied to ships going with the main tidal stream—the direction the tide moves when in flood—in this case up-channel towards the Thames estuary. Going the other way, down-channel, the green lights had to be left on the ship's port hand. But Trelle could have said to himself: Since this passage is a one-way street and you cannot travel with the main tidal stream, the lights mean what they say; they are to be passed on the mariner's starboard hand. The point may have been debatable but Trelle, if he thought of it, had little time to consider the matter. The wreck-marking vessel, however, had no alternative but to go by the internationally recognized British rule whether in a one-way channel or not.

The probable reason the *Siren* did not know of the *Brandenburg's* proximity was because Quartermaster Smith was in the radio room writing up the signal log when she went by. And, as the *Brandenburg* passed at a distance of five to six cables—over half a mile—the radar range-marker would not have sounded its alarm, it being set to respond to vessels within half a mile.

In answer to some criticism by the Sunday Times, which Trinity House challenged as "a gross distortion of the facts," the Corporation pointed out that the *Siren* was herself the warning. It added that, "We do not think our people were guilty of any dereliction of duty."

But how was it that neither the quartermaster nor anyone else heard the *Brandenburg's* horn blowing? She was still only a short distance away. Trinity House said, "Had the *Brandenburg* blown any signal on her siren, as has been alleged, it would have been heard clearly by Mr. Smith and all on board the *Siren*." Besides the quartermaster there were men on deck preparing the boats, and all testified they heard nothing. Perhaps the *Brandenburg's* horn lacked the compressed air to blow at all, or maybe emitted a feeble sound and died. As Trelle said, it's power failed before he had completed his signal. It is usually hard to recall accurately afterwards what is done in such a dreadful situation as was being encountered on the foundering *Brandenburg*.

If the *Brandenburg* had passed over the wreck at high water she would have cleared it. She sailed from Antwerp on an even keel drawing twenty-one feet. She would have had five feet to spare. But it was low water!

The reason the *Niki* did not turn away was unknown since her master and officers perished. It was surprising because Greeks were among the best of seamen. Perhaps Captain Kampitsis had not been on deck at the time but, in such a confined and busy passage, that would have been improbable. However, had he been below, the officer on watch, by watch-keeping routines at that hour, would have been the third officer—the junior.

It was a long wait but the day came, in May of the next year. The owners of the *Brandenburg* noticed that the *Paracas* had put into a British port. She had avoided doing so since the fatal night of the collision. She had been repaired and had returned to her native land and continued to trade, her Peruvian proprietors having always denied responsibility for the losses. Now Texaco Panama and Hapag Lloyd could press their claims for 'several million dollars.'

The *Paracas* had in a sense been free from extradition while on the high seas and in most foreign ports. But, perhaps thinking all had been forgotten or given up, she came up the Humber River on the sunny day of May 12, 1972, and entered the port of Hull. She was peacefully occupying a berth in the Queen Elizabeth Dock when a purposeful-looking gentleman was seen coming down the wharf. The Admiralty Marshall from the Hull Custom House strode up the gangway, crossed the deck and with deliberate care fastened a document to the ship's mainmast. He said nothing and departed. Since the crew were not well acquainted with written English they reported the event to the master who came aft and examined the formal declaration. He soon perceived that the motor vessel *Paracas* was under arrest and that Britain had entire jurisdiction over her until a certain indebtedness was discharged.

She was held in port for a week while negotiations proceeded, the outcome of which was fruitful. A guarantee was deposited with the Admiralty Court which met with the approval of the claimants' legal representatives and covered the loss of the Texaco ship and the *Brandenburg's* cargo. This was all that was demanded.

The Admiralty Marshall then removed the official instrument from the mast, and the *Paracas* sailed for Antwerp to load for Peru.